"A particular strength in the story is the delicate balance of moderation in eating and exercise as a key to deter preteens from behaviors that escalate into eating disorders in youth...I highly recommend this story to parents, preteens, and health care professionals who are eager to make positive changes toward a healthy lifestyle...This book will serve as a benchmark for professionals working with children, and an essential guide for children and families who struggle with issues involving food and inactivity." —Ann Failinger, MD, MSW, Chardon Pediatrics, Rainbow Babies and Children's Hospital

"Tweens are not quite teenagers, roughly ages 10 to 14, and they have their own set of problems. These are addressed in a fiction book for tweens, Don't Call Me Cookie....She puts her accumulated knowledge to work as a teacher and health care consultant, and by placing good advice in a framework kids will enjoy, a story." —Pat Hartman, ChildhoodObesityNews.com 11/29/2010

"Cookie shares a similar challenge to tens of thousands of young people across the country. Fortunately for her, Dr. Melvin Maximillion shares his 'not so secret' secrets about eating right and keeping 'actively active.' Appropriate for 4th to 6th graders, this helpful book is one that the parents may wish to pre-read first." —Cleveland Council of Independent Schools, Parents' Reading Room

"The message was delivered in a good way—you could connect with Cookie and her parents. While I knew what the outcome was going to be, I found myself wanting to know how she would get there. I loved the bags of vegetables—it is an idea that many kids can adopt...I love that weight loss was not portrayed as a burden, but rather as a series of small changes that build over time...I honestly think it's an excellent book. Vanessa deals with a very sensitive topic in a realistic way." —Kimberly A. Brandt, Seventh Grade Math Teacher, Hawken School

"Don't Call Me Cookie is a great book for pre-teens about living an active and healthy lifestyle. It tackles the subject in a fiction format following the life of 12 year old Cookie and her friends and family in their journey to a healthy lifestyle. The book is not overly preachy. In today's modern world, too many parents just don't get that they are poisoning their children with processed food and fast food. That may seem harsh, but I come from such a family and paid the price. My parents had good intentions but busy lives. I grew up a latch key kid that heated up too many sodium filled 'TV dinners' ...Yes, I made the choice to eat what I did, but as a kid, I wasn't purchasing the food in our house either. I would highly recommend this book to pre-teens...and their parents" —Goodreads, 11/21/2010

Don't Call Me Cookie

By Vanessa M. Pasiadis
Illustrations by Anna Lowenstein

Strategic Book Publishing and Rights Co.

Illustrated by Anna Lowenstein, Hawken School, Gates Mills, Ohio

Strategic Book Publishing and Rights Co.
12620 FM 1960, Suite A4-507
Houston, TX 77065
www.sbpra.com

ISBN: 978-1-60911-470-1

For All Children
May you learn to live healthy lives today,
So you can be "actively active" adults
tomorrow!

Contents

Acknowledgment

A sincere thank you and a great deal of credit for this book goes to our former pediatrician and respected friend, Steven C. Shapiro, MD, who currently resides in Philadelphia. A graduate of Case Western Reserve University School of Medicine and board-certified in Pediatrics, Dr. Shapiro has a long-standing interest in public health issues that affect children and their families. When I approached him to help me write this book, not only did he agree to advise me on the project, he was also generous with his time, expertise and sharing his "not-so-secret secrets" about healthful eating, green beans, and "active activity." With the original ideas for the story coming from him, together, we created:

Kate "Cookie" Lemon

Cookie Lemon   Grade 7   Ms. C. Martiss

Katherine Marie Lemon. That's my *real* name! I never hear it much. For some odd reason, everyone in my life has his or her own name for me. Actually, I answer to almost anything—except Katherine. Thanks to my buddy Justin, my friends call me "K." Grandma B.'s usual pet name for me is Missie. And, Mom and Dad...Well, that's another story!

Since the very second, I entered the world when my parents first laid eyes on me and I became their bundle of joy, they named me "Cookie." Imagine—*Cookie!* How sweet and delicious I must have looked to them! Carole and Jim Lemon saw my big eyes, round cheeks, chubby thighs, and simply decided that I should be called... Cookie.

Cookie Lemon. I'm kind of used to it—after 12 years. But, lately, I've been wondering if Mom and Dad ever thought about the person I would become or what I would look like when they gave me that name. Maybe they had dreams of me becoming a baker like Grandpa. Or, maybe they thought I'd always be "round" just like them.

If only Grandpa hadn't removed those extra syllables when he first came to this country, my life could've been a little easier—at least as far as names go. You wouldn't believe how many people chuckle about how my name could pass for an ice cream flavor. Grandma L. tells me that our original family name sort of sounds like lemonade with an "S" at the end. I guess that's not much better. That's on the foodie side too! No matter how I look at it, I'm stuck. I'm related to food!

I've been told that I take after my father, in personality and stature, and all. Aunt Linda always tells me that I am her ham—just like Dad. I love my Dad. He's a great guy. He likes to sing and dance, just like I do! I am *so* relieved they didn't come up with a name rhyming with Jim. I may be on the plump side like Daddy, but for sure, I don't look anything like a Jim. I thank my lucky stars for that!

Dad thinks my nickname is the perfect choice since he and Mom are actually convinced that I'm their *sweet* bundle of joy. It's kind of overly endearing, isn't it? I am their only child and they really are proud of me. But, enough is enough! When they are in an especially good mood, they use nicknames that are even more syrupy sounding. Who else is ever called honey bun or cupcake? It's just too embarrassing! Food! Food! Food!

My parents are horrified when my friends call me "K." So, when I turned 12 in August, I asked Mom and Dad if they could please call me Katherine or even Kate instead. I tried to tell them how much I love my real name! It sounds so regal, so cool, and so "thin." The most glamorous actresses in Hollywood have the name Katherine. Well, you would never believe how Mom and Dad answered me. They gave themselves a millisecond to think and said I could never be anyone but their scrumptious Cookie!

I'll never figure out where Mom and Dad's minds were 13 years ago. But, the more I think about this, the more I realize that "Cookie" has got to go. That's because I've *really* been looking like one lately. And, a *chunky* one, at that!

No one knows this yet, but I really want to be an actress one day. That's where I'm heading and nothing is going to stop me. Nothing; not EVEN my name.

Chapter One

The Dream

No one knows this yet. But, I really want to be an actress one day. That's where I'm heading and nothing's going to stop me. Nothing! Not even my name. Who has ever heard of a movie star named Cookie?

Kate Lemon. How awesome would that be?

Ladies and Gentlemen: Introducing the one and only...

KATE LEMON!

"Oh geez, is that the lunch bell already?" Somehow, Cookie had drifted off after finishing her English paper. She had a nasty habit of daydreaming lately—and she always felt *tired*. Well, at least her homework was done!

As she hurriedly gathered her things into her backpack, Cookie continued to think about her first English assignment of the year. How nice it was that she was already finished so it wouldn't interfere with her already-busy after-school schedule.

Ms. Martiss had assigned such a simple project and in Cookie's opinion, it was a no brainer. Each class member was asked to write about his or her own name. Since Cookie loved to make her friends laugh by making jokes about her name and size anyhow, she knew she could finish the "name" paper even in the fifteen minutes or so that Ms. Martiss allowed them in class! It just poured out of her and onto the paper—all she had left to do was type it into her computer after school!

As Cookie walked to her locker, she thought aloud about what she had written. The sound of her steps muffled her words as she mumbled under her breath. "I know I've always been plumper than most of the kids at school. I know I am teased from time to time. And I know it's one thing I joke about. I should really stop cutting myself down—it's getting really old."

Oh well, it's okay. It's just an English paper, she thought to herself, *I still have fun! I can still dream, can't I? Dreaming sure beats thinking about my silly name, I guess.*

Cookie shoved her books into her locker. Her eyes lit up when she saw her group of friends, Sara Webber, Chrissie Perkins and Justin Gordon,

waiting for her by the lunchroom. Since they were rarely scheduled in each other's classes this year, they had made an agreement to have lunch together every day. Cookie couldn't wait to tell them that she made the lead role in the middle-school play. She was so excited and rightly so! For a while, she had been lost in her own dreams of becoming a movie star. Because they'd all been friends for so long, she was sure that they would be just as happy for her.

"Hi guys!"

Chrissie, yelled back down the hall, "Hey Cookie! We heard the news! Good for you!"

Cookie was beaming. "C'mon. How did you hear about it so soon?"

Sara Webber, always having to add her own two cents in, said loudly, "News always moves around this school pretty fast. You know that."

Both Sara and Chrissie just laughed as Justin, pre-occupied with getting his soda out of the vending machine, gave each of the girls a puzzled look. Obviously, he had no clue as to why his friends were so excited. According to Sara, he was normally out of the loop. So, the girls weren't surprised when he asked, "What news? What are you talking about?"

Without giving Cookie a chance to speak, Chrissie blurted out, "Cookie got the lead! She gets to be Annie! Isn't that great?"

Justin was thrilled. *"Yes!* That's awesome! You really worked hard trying to get that part."

Justin had always been supportive of Cookie. He'd known Cookie Lemon longer than any of the others in their group. Actually, Cookie and Justin had been friends since pre-school—when they had discovered they lived around the corner from each other and shared the same late summer birthday.

They also shared a secret. From the time they were five while playing or hanging out together, Cookie often confided to Justin how silly she thought her name sounded. As the years went by, Justin noticed that this bothered Cookie more and more. One time, Cookie asked Justin if her name sounded as fat as she felt she looked. Justin didn't dare answer her question, and because he felt sorry for Cookie, he started calling her "K" for Katherine, her real name, instead. None of their friends ever knew how or why K started. But, it caught on! For fun, Cookie would call Justin, "J" from time to time. In her mind, J just sounded chummier.

Ms. Martiss, the English teacher, and everyone's favorite, picked up on their close friendship when they were both celebrating their birthdays on the first day of school. Thinking that they even looked like brother and sister, she came up with her own name for the pair. Since September, she'd been calling Cookie and Justin "the twins."

Justin looked up at Cookie, took a sip of his orange soda and said, "When you have your mind made up, you get what you want, don't you K? That's pretty cool."

"Not really. Who knows what's going to happen next week when I try out for cheerleading. I'm not going to fly like Catwoman™ with those jumps, if you know what I mean. They won't pick me. I don't think I should even bother trying out. It's way competitive. Besides, I'll be too busy with the play." Cookie didn't want them to think she expected anything.

Chrissie assuredly said, "C'mon, K. You know they'll pick you. Ms. Martiss told me that we all have a good chance."

Sara, who had no idea what kind of chances she had herself, asked Chrissie, "What makes you so sure that K will make the cut?"

"She just will, and she just has to! I know Cookie. Once she decides to do something, she always finds a way." Chrissie's confidence in Cookie's abilities showed in her smiling face. That made Cookie feel happy knowing how her friend saw her.

"You're probably right. It always seems like K gets whatever she wants. She'll probably be head cheerleader younger than anyone..." Sara replied.

Cookie, now embarrassed at being the topic of this particular discussion, interrupted Sara. "Um, hellooooo? I'm right in front of you here. Could we drop this? I'm hungry. Let's get some lunch."

But Sara was determined to get her say. "No, wait K, just hear me out. Do you remember how you were always saying you failed the test and then you got the only A-plus in the room? I mean, come on! Oh yeah, you even had us convinced that you wouldn't make the middle school play. And what do you know? You got to be Annie. We all were dying to be Annie! During tryouts, you even told me that you wouldn't have picked yourself for the role. You said that you thought you were too **big** to be Annie. Big or not, I guess you got it 'cause you sing so well."

Sara was having a hard time hiding her own envy at not being chosen as the lead.

"Sara Webber!" Justin and Chrissie couldn't believe what Sara had just said.

"I'm just repeating what K said. It's nothing we haven't heard 100 times before!"

Cookie grabbed her tray and silverware and started for the food line. Although she kept calm, Justin felt Cookie's pain and saw the hurt in her eyes.

"Sara, that was just mean! Why don't you quit while you're ahead, ok? If I were you, I'd think before opening my mouth. C'mon, let's go to lunch."

Chapter Two

The Loser Lunch Line

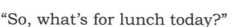

"So, what's for lunch today?"

Ms. Martiss tiptoed behind Sara Webber and grabbed Cookie's shoulders. "Is the star going to give the marvelous Ms. Martiss a cut in line?"

Cookie shrieked and giggled. "Oh, Ms. Martiss! Hi! Where did you come from? I didn't see you."

Then Sara said, "Hey Ms. Martiss. Isn't it cool that Cookie made the play?"

She was still feeling incredibly guilty about what she had said in front of the lunchroom. She really wanted Cookie to catch her compliment—indirectly or not. Sara was still was sort of proud of her and, in her own way, she wanted Cookie to know it.

Secretly, Connie Martiss was also pleased that Cookie snatched the lead. In her opinion, there really wasn't any other student that could handle the role so well. She deserved it.

Connie Martiss always thought that Cookie was such a pleasant girl and couldn't have a better group of friends. Throughout the last year or so, she had taken time to get to know them and appreciated their good nature and hard work. She liked the fact that they were all fine students and seemed to keep busy with their own individual interests and projects. So she wasn't surprised at all when she noticed how none of the kids were jealous as she continued to compliment Cookie except for maybe a twinge or two from Sara, who always thought she should be first in everything.

"I think it's *great* news, Cookie—or should I be calling you 'Annie' for the next 3 months? You're definitely going to be a very busy young lady. Between your school activities and swim team, your evenings will be rather booked, if I may say so myself. I heard that you're also trying out for next year's cheerleading group. Good for you!"

"Thanks, Ms. Martiss. I'll definitely be busy. But, I'll get everything in—you'll see. I might have more time because I don't know if I want to try out for cheerleading. It's not for me. I'm even wondering if I should take a break from swimming too."

Connie Martiss didn't expect Cookie to be so doubtful and tried her best not to show her disappointment. However, she did try to convince her to stick with all of her physical activities. She remembered Cookie and her friends walking through the school halls last year. On the first day of this new school year, Ms. Martiss especially noticed that both Cookie and Justin had each added a few pounds and appeared a little chunkier than before. She felt badly for them and sincerely didn't want to see any young person frustrated with their weight. She knew all about that. She'd been there before.

Connie Martiss had always been a chubby child and a heavy adult. Because of her sense of humor and friendly nature, the kids would never guess this about her in a million years. There was a time before she interviewed for the 7th grade English teacher position that she had been at least forty pounds heavier. Since she'd taught at the middle school, Ms. Martiss had even managed to lose a few more pounds simply by eating healthy foods and keeping physically active. She decided that coaching and working out with the cheerleading squad would be another great way to help her stay fit. Ms. Martiss also knew that keeping a food diary was a sure way to "help think about the feelings and reasons for overeating." She sometimes toyed with the idea of having her students keep a food diary just to show them how to eat healthfully. She just wasn't sure how to introduce this concept into an English class. She was going to have to figure that one out!

"Cookie—listen to me. Don't stop the swimming. You know what they say about getting things done. The busiest people get everything in. Keep doing what you're doing. You'll feel great. You'll see—you'll be just fine." Ms. Martiss smiled encouragingly at her student and was about to suggest a couple of ideas for Cookie when Chrissie Perkins jumped in line, grabbed her tray and abruptly interrupted Ms. Martiss. "Hey Ms. Martiss. Our paper's due tomorrow, isn't it?" The moment was lost.

"Whoa Chris! Slow down. Yes—to answer your question, it actually *is* due tomorrow for everyone except for the students in the fourth period. Lucky you! Your class gets off the hook. Mr. Eaton scheduled an assembly during your class' English period."

"No...really? You're kidding, aren't you?"

Connie Martiss loved keeping her students guessing. She laughed and said, "No kidding this time. Consider it your gift for the week. Everyone in your class gets an extra bonus day to work on the paper. Now...no excuses! Fourth period English students should only be turning in wonderfully creative papers. Right?"

Even though Justin seemed to be intensely deciding between the shriveled up pizza and the rubbery grilled cheese sandwich, he certainly wasn't going to let the comment about Sara's class getting an extra day for the paper pass him by.

"Wait a minute! That's not fair! Why couldn't the assembly be scheduled during first period when I have English?"

Ms. Martiss looked over her glasses and scolded Justin. "Aren't you even going to say 'Hello' first, Justin Gordon?" She shook her head as she continued down the lunch line with her tray and lectured the students behind her. "You *all* need a course on good manners. I haven't heard one 'Excuse me or Pardon me!' No...sometimes, life isn't fair. Don't worry. You'll get your 'free lunch' someday too. However, I expect to see *your* paper tomorrow. Speaking of lunch, what are they serving today?"

Turned off by what she saw being served at lunch, Sara whispered to Cookie, "Forget **what** they're serving. The question is—**when** will they serve something that we can actually eat? This stuff's horrible. This pizza looks like it's going to fail the napkin test. The green beans look gross, too. They're **always** gross! Who eats green beans with pizza anyways? Oh well, it looks like it is pop and rolls again—at least for now. I guess I'll be eating chicken nuggets at the mall after school, or I'll never make it to dinner."

Ms. Martiss couldn't help but overhear what Sara was telling Cookie in the lunch line. "Sara, what in the world is the napkin test?"

Cookie proudly answered the question for Sara. "Ms. Martiss, don't you know? Placing a clean napkin on top of a slice of pizza tests the amount of grease. If the napkin's really greasy, then the pizza is way too greasy to eat. If the napkin is greasy in certain spots, then the pizza passes the napkin test. That never happens. At this school, the pizza always fails the test. No one wants to eat dry pizza. Overly

greasy pizza is disgusting too. So...on pizza days no one eats anything—except the fries."

"That's terrible. And does that mean that none of you eat a good lunch?" Ms. Martiss couldn't help commenting. "Don't any of you use the salad bar? It's a great one. There's nothing but delicious fresh fruit and crispy vegetables."

Justin Gordon answered for the group. "Sure we eat lunch, if it's decent. But today, it isn't. So I'm only having fries, pop, and ice cream. Usually, if we're lucky, some of us get our Moms to take us to the food court at the mall for an after-school snack before we head off to music lessons or sports anyhow."

He turned and looked over at the salad bar on the other side of the room. "Yuck! How can anyone eat that stuff on that salad bar? Eating raw vegetables to me is like eating cotton. Have you ever tried to eat cotton? It's miserable! Just awful!"

Ms. Martiss rolled her eyes and decided that she was better off keeping quiet for the time being. She had said enough for the day. Besides, she had to move quickly with her lunch because she had two parent conference calls to handle when she was finished. It just so happened that one of the calls was about overhearing another group of kids teasing Justin. Of all students! Poor thing. She was appalled when she saw them imitating him before a swim practice.

What she saw happened by accident...

Ms. Martiss turned the corner by the pool and stopped when she overheard Sam Willis and Mikey Downey talking.

"They should just call him "Mr. J" for "Mr. Jiggles," Sam laughed, and started imitating Justin's walk.

"Yeah," Mikey replied, laughing too. "Do you ever notice how his thighs rub together? He could start a fire!" Ms. Martiss listened as the boys continued to tease and laugh, adding comments about how his stomach hung over his Speedos when he got out of the pool. Justin, still changing in the locker room, thankfully never heard. Otherwise, he would've been devastated...

That wasn't the first time Connie Martiss had heard such thoughtless teasing. During recess over a week or so ago, she also witnessed the same boys bugging Justin on the playground and calling him "Justin the Jiggler." He really wasn't as heavy as they were making him out to be. She could only guess that these boys had to be jealous of Justin's swimming ability and strength. After all, despite his size, he was the fastest swimmer on the team.

Kids can be so mean, she thought to herself and sighed. She wanted to settle this issue immediately.

Also baffled by what the school offered for lunch, Connie Martiss looked down at her students in line and announced, "I'm checking out the salad bar. Oh...for your information Mr. Justin...I love it! You don't know what you're missing. There's some great stuff over there. Trust me, you should try it sometime."

Before leaving the line, she paused and added, "By the way, I'm sure you all wouldn't mind if I changed the subject. However...if you're interested, don't forget that cheerleading tryouts are in two weeks from today. This year, the school wants both boys and girls to participate. Remember...you can't try out without a permission slip signed by your doctor. See you later, guys. Have a good afternoon."

Speaking for her friends, Cookie said, "See you later, Ms. Martiss. Thanks."

As Ms. Martiss walked her tray over to other side of the room, Cookie couldn't help but notice how slim her teacher appeared compared to when she first saw her after the summer break on the first day of school.

Chapter Three

The Reflection

Cookie threw her coat onto the banister in the back hallway and dropped her bulging book bag next to the lineup of shoes that cluttered the corner. She was exhausted and couldn't believe that it was already 5:30. The day had gone by so quickly—but it had to be the best day in her life. She made the play. She was actually given the lead role. Incredible! This probably never happened to a seventh grader before. Nothing like this had ever happened to **her** before. Thinking about her first rehearsal and the excitement of the months ahead, she walked into the kitchen and saw her Mom's note posted on the refrigerator door. Cookie was disappointed when she learned that she wasn't able to share her great news with her parents for at least another hour. She was used to no one at home after school. Tonight she really wanted them here. Of all times to plan to be later than usual! Dad had a doctor's appointment and Mom had a community board meeting. Unbelievable!

Absolutely starved, Cookie opened the pantry and scanned the shelves for what she thought was a decent enough snack to hold her over until dinner. She grabbed a handful of Oreos, danced over to the refrigerator, and poured herself a glass of milk. Because she was feeling just so wonderful, Cookie burst out with the tune from *Annie.* She twirled around the kitchen table and danced back over to the breakfast bar. After a minute or so, she stopped singing when she realized that Mr. Cat was her only audience. She felt so foolish.

Imagine if my friends saw me entertaining my cat!

She laughed at herself, created a makeshift megaphone with her hands, and hollered, "Earth calling the one and only Cookie Lemon. Get back to reality *ASAP!*"

Cookie bent over to give Mr. Cat a rub. Unfortunately, "the show" had to end. She was immediately reminded of her evening's work when she saw the stuffed backpack leaning in the corner. The tired new 'star' begrudgingly picked up the sack of books, grabbed a few more cookies, and dragged herself up the stairs to her bedroom with Mr. Cat following behind her. All she could think of was how her excitement was ruined because she had to spend the rest of the evening doing homework. She looked down at the cat and said, "I have 12 more" think and review" math questions to do. Luckily, all I have to do is type and print that English paper. This is going to be a *long* night."

Cookie couldn't believe Chrissie's luck. She had another day to finish the assignment—and she didn't even have to go to play rehearsal. Cookie had really tried her best to type the paper in the library but all the computers and printers were taken. Cookie wanted an "A" badly and she was determined to get it. This was going to take some time. First, she had to get those review problems out of the way. She had the perfect solution!

I'll give Justin a call. I think he finished his work sheet in study hall this morning. Maybe he can give me a few freebees. He owes me one.

Cookie placed her glass of milk and cookies on her desk and dumped her books and spiral notebooks from the backpack onto her bed. She sat cross-legged on the bed and decided to reread the English paper from this morning. She had really enjoyed writing it. It felt good to get her emotions about her name out there. Maybe when she typed it up, she would start a journal or a blog to share with her friends. Who knew she liked to write?

With the cat snuggling next to her, Cookie read and reread the last line she had remembered writing as she drifted off into one of her daydreams again...

A chunky one at that!

Cookie shuddered at her thoughts as she imagined the only possible acting job in her future.

I guess I could be a commercial actress for a cookie company. I'd be perfect! And I wouldn't even have to wear a big, FAT cookie costume.

Not knowing how to continue, she leaned over the cat and picked up the cell phone hidden under the magazines piled on her bed stand to call her friend. She looked at Mr. Cat and said, "He's got to help me with the math stuff. Please, Justin Gordon. Please be home."

Cookie punched his number only to get a busy signal on the other end. "Oh good, at least someone's there."

Cookie thought she'd try again in a few minutes. She absently clicked off the phone, lifted her head, and caught her face in the mirror across from the foot of her bed. She met her eyes in the mirror and gazed at the face that returned her stare. She thought for a moment and wondered why she always made fun of herself. "I've always looked like this," she mumbled. "It's a never-ending battle." She really took a good look at herself. She *was* getting heavier and heavier. Her clothes just didn't fit right anymore. Yesterday in gym class, she noticed her shorts riding up into her crotch whenever she walked. Swim practice after school was even worse! She made it *absolutely mandatory* that a towel be wrapped around her waist whenever she was not in the pool. Bathing suits were the worst things ever invented.

But I LOVE to swim. What else am I supposed to wear?

Cookie leaned back onto her pillow and continued to think. Lately it seemed that every morning she agonized over whether or not she should step on that scale in her parents' bathroom. Every night at dinner all she heard was her Mom making comments about the *clean plate club* and not eating in between meals.

Still, she forces me to eat everything on my plate— even if I'm 100% stuffed!

Cookie sipped some milk and thought about her Grandma. Unlike her Mom, she would give her 'Missy' her favorite dessert even if she didn't finish her dinner.

But that never happens. I always finish my dinner. How could I not? Granny's the greatest cook. She loves to call me her best eater. Now, she talks about how "well-fed" I'm looking these days. Is that why I heard her whispering to Mom about how she needed to check into a kid version of plus sizes?

She knew they were talking about her. Even her best friends were talking about her size.

Everyone was talking about her!

Best eater. Plus sizes for girls. Kids at school...

Cookie pushed a strand of hair away from her eye and became uncomfortable with what she saw in the mirror. She looked at herself.

What am I going to do? Who should I talk with? This is so embarrassing. Mom just says, 'Don't worry, Honey. You'll grow out of it.' How funny! She never had to worry

about it! Granny tells me to keep eating healthy food. 'It's good for your brain.' Right! Now tell me, how can that creamy rice pudding that she makes me be good for my brain?

Cookie became frustrated and upset. She lifted the cat from her lap and stepped over her school papers that toppled onto the floor as she moved from the bed. Then Cookie went to stand directly in front of the mirror. She took a good, LONG look at her reflection and repeatedly voiced the words that she put into writing, "A chunky one at that! I look like I eat cookies. Look at me. I look like I LOVE to eat cookies, don't I?"

Mr. Cat happened to purr at that very second. Cookie swiftly turned around, glared, and said, "Who gave *you,* of all things, permission to agree with me?"

Cookie went over to hug her cat and started to cry, "What am I going to do? I love to eat and it shows. C'mon, Cookie! You're just tired. Get with the program and do your work."

She wiped her eyes, went to her bed stand, and redialed Justin's number. No busy signal this time. "Hello Mrs. Gordon, this is Cookie. Is Justin there?"

"Hi Cookie. Sure, hang on a minute. Oh, Cookie...Are you okay?"

"Sure. I'm great. Why?"

"You sound like you've been crying. I hope not. Anyhow, Justin told me that you made *Annie.* That's really great news. Congratulations!"

"Thanks Mrs. Gordon. I think it's going to be lots of fun. I can't wait 'til my parents know. Did Justin tell you how much homework we have?"

"It seems like quite a bit, especially since the two of you are so busy. Let me get him for you. Have a good night."

Justin picked up the phone in the study. "Hi there, K."

"Hey, J. I tried to reach you about 10 minutes ago and your line was busy."

"Mom was on the phone. For some reason, Ms. Martiss left a message when we were at school this afternoon. Mom just got home and had to call her back. I don't know what that was all about. She didn't look happy though. Hope I'm not in trouble or something. Oh well. What's up?"

"I really need your help with the review problems for math. Can you at least give me the answers to the odd questions? I know how to do these. So, I'm not *really* cheating. I just don't have the time. I still have to type up Ms. Martiss' paper. Are you done?"

Justin let out a big sigh and said, "Almost. That was more work than I thought. How did Chrissie get to be the one to have an extra night to finish this stuff? I'm finally typing the last paragraph on the computer. Wait a sec. Let me get the math sheet."

Cookie and Justin exchanged questions, and briefly chuckled about Sara Webber's latest crush. Finally, they realized that they had better get some work done before dinner.

"Thanks, J. I better let you go. I still have to type the paper. Silly me, I should've started it yesterday at home on my computer. I would've been done by now. See you tomorrow at lunch."

"See ya. Oh…don't forget that it's a swimming day in gym class tomorrow."

"Yeah, that's just what I needed to hear! Oh well, I guess I'll see you then."

Cookie hung up the phone and was relieved. "Good. I can finish the rest of the problems tomorrow in homeroom. Now, I have to attack that paper! Hopefully, I can wrap it up before dinner."

Chapter Four

The Fateful Fall

Cookie sat down at the computer and in a short while had typed the paper and printed it neatly to hand in to Ms. Martiss. Since her math was done, she found herself with a few moments, so she opened a new document on her laptop and started to write:

> I think that keeping a journal is a great way to let ME know what is going on with me. Today has been a day of really mixed emotions! I am the LEAD in ANNIE! But every time I look in the mirror all I see is a chunky Cookie looking back. That's all I needed. I don't want to get up on stage and have everyone looking at me because I am the first plus sized Annie in history! I just don't know what to do about it. Maybe that salad bar at school will help. Who am I kidding? I am never going to look like Sara Webber!

She leaned over her desk, lifted a corner of the curtain, and peeked out the window. She wondered what was keeping them.

The clock on the bed stand read that it was shortly before 8:00. It was much later than she thought. She usually didn't mind being home alone. Both of her parents had worked forever. After so many years of the routine, Cookie was somewhat comfortable with their unpredictable schedule. Tonight was different! She wanted so badly to talk to someone about her day.

She thought about her grandmother again. Oh, how she missed her—especially now. Before Cookie turned 12, Grandma B. had lived a little closer. It was easier than for her grandmother to drop by and greet her after school. She loved talking about Cookie's day and about the kids at school. On each visit Grandma B. brought with her a fully cooked homemade dinner. When she had the extra time, she spoiled Cookie's family with her wonderfully delicious sausage and pork spaghetti sauce and her super creamy rice pudding for dessert. That was when coming home was *really* special! Nowadays, Cookie couldn't remember the last time when she didn't have a frozen meal or "take-out" for dinner on a school night.

Still, Grandma phoned every other evening from her new apartment in the retirement village on the other side of town. But it wasn't the same. She was getting too old to make the trip to Cookie's house. She was always too busy worrying about Grandpa Ed. Since he had his stroke, Cookie only saw her grandmother a few times a month—usually on a Sunday.

Thankfully, Mr. Cat kept her company now. Once her homework was done she and Mr. Cat would cuddle on the couch and watch afternoon TV shows together. There was always Justin. When the weather was nice, sometimes Mrs. Gordon let them meet halfway on their bikes to follow each other to the neighborhood store to buy candy. On a "homework-free" night, Cookie might even get together with her friends at either Chrissie or Sara's house. When they weren't sitting around and swapping stories about the kids at school, they were usually playing their favorite video games. Life could have been far worse being alone.

This evening though, the time just whizzed by! Cookie was relieved she had finished her paper and started her journal. Justin was so great to have given her a hand with those math problems. She was now able to relax for the rest of the evening, eat dinner with her parents, and tell them about her role as *Annie*. She couldn't wait!

At last, Cookie heard the rolling sound of the garage door opening beneath her bedroom. She went back over to the window and was so surprised to see her mother's car pulling into the garage. Usually her father was home first.

Actually, Jim Lemon was usually home early enough to help Cookie set the table and sort the mail with 10 or 15 minutes to spare to check his daughter's math problems. Carole Lemon never got home before 7:00—at least a half hour or so after her husband! Her gazillion *after work* stops kept her from ending her day any sooner. Cookie knew her mother like the back of her hand. She got caught up in small talk with someone wherever she went—and Carole Lemon was sure to make friends with everyone!

Hearing her mother's footsteps entering the house, Cookie quickly organized her work and notebooks for the next day. As she was picking up the papers from her bed and repacking her book bag, she pressed her hand against her stomach to stifle the grumbling sounds coming from her body.

The gurgling noises were loud enough to cause Mr. Cat to pounce from the dresser top onto the bed next to where she was sitting. Cookie stopped for a moment. She leaned the zipped-up backpack against the leg of her desk, looked down at her cat, and said, "This is so weird. How could I be so hungry so soon?"

Cookie remembered getting off the phone and running down into the kitchen to put her dirty dishes in the dishwasher. She recalled grabbing an unopened bag of chips from the pantry and searching the refrigerator for something cold to drink. The cookies she had eaten earlier made her thirsty. Then she had run back up the stairs with the bag in one hand and a liter of cherry cola in another.

She looked down and noticed the crumbled, empty bag next to the hollow, plastic pop bottle in the trash. Cookie had no idea that she had finished the entire bag, or the bottle, for that matter. It had dawned on her that she ate the last chip as she was wrapping up her homework. She must've been hungry!

Cookie picked up Mr. Cat and started heading for her door. Hopefully, her Mom had something good for dinner. As she was leaving her room, she heard her mother's high voice.

"Cookie...Sweetie Pie, I'm home." Carole Lemon called up the stairs to her daughter.

Mrs. Lemon hung her coat in the back hallway closet and continued shouting her conversation as she walked into the kitchen to unload her groceries. "Sorry I'm late. I just ran into Sara's Mom at the store! She told me some terrific news!"

Hearing what her mother was about to tell her, Cookie sprinted through the hallway with the cat in her arms and jumped down the stairs two at a time. Cookie couldn't believe that her mother already knew about *Annie*. She wanted to be the first one to surprise her. She was excited all day and now not anymore! "I can't believe you heard about the play already. I wanted to be the first one to tell you. I could've been—if *you* hadn't come home so late! Why did you take so long to come home? Where were you?"

Cookie started to cry. She was so hurt and terribly upset that her parents weren't home on such a special day. She forgot her usual role as the obedient daughter and continued to lecture her mother as she headed down the stairs towards the kitchen. "If you weren't always talking to 50,000 people you wouldn't have been late again. *You ruined it for me!* You're so worried about everyone else all the time! You should be more concerned about your own daughter and your own family and *not* be such a busybody! Everybody thinks you're a *busybody! Just ask Mrs. Gordon!"*

Carole Lemon was beside herself! Her daughter had never spoken to her like this before. She had never ever seen her so upset before either. Something else really had to be bothering her! *"Katherine Marie Lemon! How dare you talk to me in that tone! You better get downstairs and apologize right now!"*

Without looking where she was going, Cookie tripped over a pair of sneakers left on the middle step.

Oh no! I forgot to take those shoes to my room!

She lost her balance, skipped over the last set of risers and landed flat on her bottom with her ankle twisted beneath her. Mr. Cat flew out of her hands and flopped right on top of her chest. She was trying to balance herself. But it didn't work.

Cookie's Mom heard the thud and ran to her daughter, who was slowly and painfully trying to pick herself up from the floor. *"You owe me that apology young lady! Get over here..."*

Carole Lemon stopped shouting when she turned the corner and noticed her daughter looking up with a strained look on her face and tears in her eyes. "Cookie! Honey Bun! What happened? Are you okay?"

As Mr. Cat wiggled free from her hold, Cookie winced and began to sob.

"I can't believe you heard about the play. I wanted to be the first one to tell you. Why did you take so long to come home? Why isn't Daddy home yet?"

Carole Lemon really did think her husband would be home by now. She was surprised that he wasn't. He only had a simple doctor's appointment. She wondered what was keeping him.

Carole Lemon bent over to help Cookie up from the floor. When she realized that her daughter was truly injured, she did her best to hold her temper and gently placed her arms around her shoulder to try to lift her up.

Cookie's ankle throbbed as she was trying to stand upright with her mother's help. "Ohhh. Ouch! I think I did something to my foot! I can't step on it without it really hurting."

"Oh Cookie! What *did* you do? It had to be that tennis shoe. I've been tripping on that thing all week!"

She leaned against her mother and carefully hopped over to the table to sit on one of the kitchen chairs. Carole Lemon slowly lifted her daughter's foot onto another chair and turned to walk over to the freezer to quickly search for an ice pack. "Let me see. We never have anything when we need it. Of course, I can't find an ice pack right now. I guess this will do." She pulled a sack of frozen peas from one of the shelves, hurried back over to where Cookie sat and secured it around Cookie's bruised ankle with a dishtowel.

Cookie moaned as her mother adjusted her foot.

"Don't move. The coldness from the frozen sack should keep the swelling down. I know it hurts. To me, it looks like you can move your ankle and foot pretty well. Maybe you didn't injure yourself so badly after all."

Carole Lemon walked back over to the kitchen counter and continued unloading the bags she was carrying into the house. She turned to her daughter who looked noticeably upset and said, "We have to give this some time. Sit there for a few minutes and talk to me while I get our dinner ready."

As she took the food out of the cartons, Carole Lemon was thinking about how she was going to reschedule her morning. She had a feeling that a good part of the next day was going to be spent between visiting Dr. Max, the town pediatrician, and the radiology department at the hospital. For sure, Dr. Max would want a picture of that ankle. From her point of view, the swelling only appeared to be getting worse. How was she going to break this news to her daughter?

She sampled a remaining crispy crunchy fry. "Mmm. This is *so* good. They had the super dinner on special today. Extra fries were included. Isn't that terrific?"

Carole Lemon divided the fried chicken drumsticks and thighs onto three separate plates. Then she piled on a generous serving of the store's famous crispy, crunchy fries, creamy coleslaw and two flaky, buttered rolls. Homemade or not, she liked having a hearty dinner ready when her husband walked through the door. "Knowing that I was going to be late, I picked up your favorite fried chicken and potato meal on my way home from my meeting."

Cookie then watched her mother pick apart an extra piece of the chicken, place it in her mouth, and lick her fingers. "Oh—this is delicious chicken.

It's too good to wait for. I'm sure Daddy will be walking in the door any minute, so let's just eat now. We can always have seconds with him when he comes in. Besides, eating a little something will help you feel better. You'll see."

Cookie didn't think the chicken would make her feel better at all. She had lost her appetite. She couldn't tell if it was because she was in so much pain or if she simply wasn't hungry anymore. She did know one thing for sure—watching her Mom pick on the chicken pieces reminded her of her own bad habits. After all, she ate enough of an after-school snack for three people. Only on her Mom, it never showed. She could eat just about anything and never gain weight. It's not that she was skinny but she always appeared trim—even if she rarely exercised or kept fit.

Carole Lemon brought the dinner plates over to the table. She folded the napkins, placed the silverware, and poured them each a glass of juice. She sat across from her daughter, looked her squarely in the eyes, and said, "Now, let's start all over again. I understand that you had a wonderful day. Tell me how you found out about your good news."

Even though she was angry and uncomfortable, Cookie still decided to share her success about getting the lead role in *Annie* with her mother. Nothing else had made her feel so special in a long time!

Chapter Five

The Disastrous Dinner

Jim Lemon loosened his tie under his coat as he meandered from the car to the side kitchen door of his home. He looked up at the sky and took a deep breath. It was crystal clear. Not a single cloud. The night was brisk. It just felt so refreshing to be outside for even a short while. There couldn't be a better evening to go for a walk.

He was exhausted. The workday was busy. Waiting over an hour to see Dr. Morgan was trying. However, hearing his warnings about heart disease and diabetes was what really got the best of him. Jim Lemon had no idea that his blood pressure was so high. He never imagined that he was more than fifty pounds overweight! He never realized that he was eating so many wrong things. His diet had always been his wife's department. It didn't seem to affect her weight. How one person could eat everything and not gain weight and someone else eat the same stuff and put on an extra fifty pounds! The good doctor was right. Some things in his life would have to change or he'd be in deep trouble. It didn't seem fair, but there it was.

He heard his daughter's laughter as he unlocked the side door. It was music to his ears! He thought that maybe after dinner Cookie could walk with him and share part of her day. Nothing could make Jim Lemon happier.

Usually they caught up while making their special dessert sundaes together. That kind of dessert would have to change. After his rather frightful session with the doctor, he decided that walking should be their evening activity from now on.

"Hi, girls. Sorry I'm so late." He hung his coat in the closet, dropped his briefcase next to the back step, and walked over to the sink to wash his hands. "Mmm. It smells so good in here. What did you slave over a hot stove making tonight?"

Carole Lemon rolled her eyes. "Very funny, Mr. Lemon. You know I'm a great cook, and with more time, I'd have a nice homemade meal for you." She got up from the table and placed his covered dish in the microwave.

"Oh Carole, I'm kidding." He gave her a big hug and stepped over to the table to kiss his daughter on her forehead before taking his seat at the end. He was so worried about his day that he didn't notice Cookie's swollen eyes or propped-up leg that was carefully supported by the chair under the table. "Looks like you gals have started eating. Hm, fried chicken tonight, huh?"

Carole didn't catch her husband's concerned look. "Mmm. You bet. There was a special on the super meal today. I picked it up to surprise Cookie. She had such a great day; I thought she'd enjoy the treat." Carole Lemon placed the warmed plate in front of her husband, filled his glass with cola, and took the seat next to him. "Go ahead, sweetie. Tell Daddy your good news."

Cookie's eyes and face lit up as she started telling her father how she made the lead role in the middle-school play.

"Wonderful! What terrific news! Congratulations! That's the best news I've heard in months!" Being the actor that he was, Jim Lemon rose from the table, dramatically sashayed over to his daughter and pulled her up from the chair. As he attempted to give her a hug, Cookie let out a huge scream.

"*Don't!*"

At the same time, the towel slipped off Cookie's ankle and the bag of peas fell hard on to the floor. Within two seconds, more than a hundred defrosted peas had rolled in every possible direction.

Jim Lemon didn't know if he was more disturbed by the avalanche of peas or by his daughter's painful squeal. "What in the world is going on here?"

He looked down at her ankle and answered his own question. "Will someone tell me what happened?"

Carole didn't give her daughter a chance to speak. She was so disturbed with the evening's sequence of events that she immediately went into describing Cookie's accident. In the meantime, she was on her hands and knees carefully picking up the dropped peas, pushing Mr. Cat out of her way and shaking her head.

When the last escaped pea was rounded up, Jim helped his wife up from the floor and started to lecture his daughter. "Cookie, I've tripped over those shoes a dozen times myself!"

Cookie took a deep breath and let out a sob as she told her side of the story.

"I was so excited to tell you about making the play. I was so patient. I waited all day! I even finished all of my homework. You were both so late! Justin and Mrs. Gordon are happier for me—more than you could ever be!"

"Now wait just a minute, young lady. You're not being fair to us. Let's get back to the dinner table and talk about why I was so late this evening. I think I have pretty important news to share too."

Cookie leaned on her father's arm as she hopped back over to her chair. "You really are in pain, aren't you? It's such a perfect fall evening. I really wanted to go on a walk with you tonight. So much for that idea."

After a few calmer moments, Carole looked up and realized that she was the only one eating. Her daughter was pushing her food around the plate and her husband hadn't even lifted his fork. "Isn't anyone hungry? Or are you both too upset to eat? I really thought you'd enjoy this dinner tonight. It's so delicious!"

Jim Lemon folded his arms and addressed his wife in a very solemn voice,

"Carole, I had a very serious meeting with Dr. Morgan this evening. He shared the test results of last week's appointment and pretty much told me that I was in bad shape. He said that if I wasn't careful, I was a heart attack waiting to happen. He told me to start exercising and to watch what I eat. That's why I wanted to go for a walk. He especially mentioned how I should stay away from food like this and eat more fruit, vegetables, and fish. He even showed me a picture of what my arteries would look like if I continue to eat much more of this fried stuff. It's pretty bad..."

For once, Carole was speechless. She knew that her husband enjoyed eating food like fried chicken, corned beef and banana cream pie. She always wanted to please him. Since it was hard for her to find the time to cook, Carole Lemon just found it more convenient to pick up her husband's favorite meals on her way home from work. She never gave it a second thought. She never imagined what he loved to eat could be so unhealthy! Now what would she do? The last thing she wanted was for him to go hungry!

Knowing how empty her refrigerator had been, Carole decided that the only quick meal she could put together was a fruit salad. She left her dinner, walked over to the refrigerator and took out an apple, a few oranges, and the half-emptied container of cottage cheese.

Jim Lemon couldn't grasp what his wife was doing. "Why are you up? C'mon, sit down and finish your meal before it gets too cold."

Carole made the fruit salad and placed it in front of her husband. In a determined and very concerned voice, she said, "No, Jim. I can't watch you eat something that could be so bad for you. I just never thought about how unhealthy we've been eating. There's no better time to change than now. I don't know about you, but I want you around to walk your daughter down the aisle."

Cookie was also upset about the serious news her father had shared with them. After hearing his words, she was immediately reminded of Ms. Martiss' comments in the afternoon. There must be an epidemic! Even *she* was talking about healthy eating, vegetables, and salad bars.

Now all Cookie could think about was how awful she still felt from eating all of those cookies and chips after school. Maybe that's what caused her to become so tired and frustrated as she waited and waited for her mother. The injured ankle just made things worse. It had made her feel even *more* uncomfortable.

The family started back into their meals and continued with their conversation about the doctor's visit. The mood became a little lighter when Jim Lemon started highlighting the better parts of his day. As he was speaking, he noticed that his daughter was lost in thought. He glanced over at her foot resting on the extra chair and said, "Hey, Cupcake, it looks like we're going to have to pay a visit to Dr. Max in the morning. You've got a real bruise there."

Cookie didn't want to take any chances and miss anything important in school. "Oh Dad, do I have to go tomorrow? It's so hard to be absent—even for a half-day. There's always too much to make up. I'll be okay...really. Justin will help me with my books through the day. I know he will."

Cookie was in denial. In her mind, the ankle was just fine. She even schemed—*if it begins to feel worse, I'll have Dr. Max look at it during my cheerleading physical next week.*

Actually, she didn't mind her visits to Dr. Melvin Maximillion, the town pediatrician. He was a nice guy—at least from a kid's point of view. Everyone seemed to call him Dr. Max. He was a portly man with a nice cool voice and a sense of humor. But *that nurse,* Ms. Liz! She was the bothersome one. She always said something to you that hurt—even if it was by accident.

She could hear her heavily accented Scottish voice right now..."*My, my young lady, almost eight pounds since you were here last.*"

"Cookie, Cookie...helloooo! Are you daydreaming again?"

Stretching the truth, Cookie replied. "No Mom. I was really thinking how I don't want to miss school."

Carole looked at her daughter and realized that she still wasn't eating her dinner. "You're not going to tell me that *you* don't want to eat either. You're too young to be removing such great tasting food from your diet. You're a growing girl. Everything's good for you! Come on. Finish up. Guess what? I picked up some pastry for us to enjoy for dessert." Carole Lemon never really worried about her weight—she always could eat everything and she taught her daughter all about the same foods she loved as a child. It didn't hurt her, so why should it affect Cookie?

Remembering her husband's health situation, Carole Lemon looked over at him and said, "Oh, I almost forgot. I have a cup of tea for you dear, okay?"

Always trying to please, Cookie hurriedly finished eating everything on her plate—even though she was still full from her after-school snacking. She knew she could only get dessert if she finished her meal. She certainly didn't want to pass up dessert tonight. She had a sneaking suspicion that it would be her absolute favorite—chocolate cream pie! Her Mom always bought her chocolate cream pie on special occasions.

After dinner, Jim helped his wife clear the dishes and together they discussed how they were going to handle the morning. With his flexible schedule, he decided that it would be better if he took his daughter to see Dr. Max. He returned to the table and knelt in front of his daughter. "Cookie, I'll be the one to take you to the doctor's tomorrow morning. Be glad that you're up to date with all of your work. Think about it, sweetie. If something's very wrong with your foot, you could have some trouble keeping up with your musical practices. We have no choice but to check this out now, or you'll never be healed enough to sing and dance on the stage."

"Oh no! I have to be in that play! I've never wanted something so much in my life! What about cheerleading tryouts? And what am I supposed to do about swimming? Ms. Martiss will really be disappointed if I stop swimming!"

Carole calmed her daughter down. "That's why we're taking you to the doctor's." She glanced at the stove clock. "It's really late...after 9:30. You've had quite a day and are in need of a good night's rest. Come on now, let Daddy and me help you up the stairs."

After her parents tucked her into bed and kissed her goodnight, she laid awake thinking about her day. How could it go from being so wonderful and exciting to being so gloomy? How could she be so happy one moment and so sad the next? Her stomach ached and her ankle really, really hurt! What if it didn't get better? Hopefully, Dr. Max would have good news.

Chapter Six

The Waiting Room

"*Daaddyy!*! Everyone's looking at us! *Puhleeze!*! I can walk from the parking lot." Cookie was SO embarrassed when her Dad pulled their car up onto the curb and as close as three feet from the doctor's office entrance.

"C'mon Dad! You're always so dramatic!"

Jim Lemon shook his head and pretended that he didn't hear her. This morning, he had only one mission. He had to get his daughter in to see Dr. Max A.S.A.P.

After seeing Cookie suffer and stumble this morning, he knew very well that she couldn't walk another foot. He was amazed that he even got her to this appointment on time. It seemed like hours watching her hobble from the kitchen to the bathroom at the end of the back hallway just to brush her teeth. Because things were creeping along, he thought it was best that she skip breakfast. Jim Lemon never saw the point of eating breakfast anyhow. In his mind, it was just a waste of time. If she had eaten those bacon and eggs like her mother wanted, they would've been over ten minutes late.

He left the engine running and hurried to open the passenger door. "Grab my arm and I'll help you up. Stand on your good foot first and we'll hop right inside the doctor's office." He opened the door and carefully guided his daughter to the closest chair. "Sit here while I park the car. I'll be right back."

Cookie sat patiently waiting for her Dad to return. She picked up an old issue of the *Highlights for Children,* the kids' magazine filled with stories and puzzles. As she flipped through it, she peeked over the pages and secretly stole a few glances at Ms. Liz sitting at her desk in front of the little window.

The nurse had to know that she was there. After all, Cookie saw her look up from her paperwork when her Dad first brought her in.

Why couldn't she say "hello?"

Cookie placed the tattered magazine back onto the pile on the table, took a good look around the room, and realized that everything was the same as it was at last year's visit.

She took a deep breath and decided that it even smelled the same. How could she forget that medicine-like odor? The overgrown plants were still in the corner. The sign-in book had that fat, red pen attached to it by the black string. And those same pictures were still hanging on the opposite walls.

Oh those pictures! Cookie always thought they were stupid, but each time she visited, she couldn't help but stare at them.

I can't believe Dr. Max still has these silly people made of fruit and vegetables framed in his waiting room.

Cookie looked carefully at the print over the aquarium on the left side of the room. It appeared that the lady in the picture had all of the features of

Mrs. Potato Head—without the potato. It seemed that her head was an apple; her hands were celery stalks and her legs looked like carrots. Her body was actually a head of lettuce.

A head of lettuce? What a strange looking lady!

Cookie wanted to walk over to the picture and examine it more closely. Knowing that she'd have to hop over on one foot, she decided that it wouldn't be such a great idea. The last thing she needed was to get Ms. Liz's attention. So she sat straight in her chair, stretched her neck, and focused on the funny lady's eyes, mouth, and ears. She became even more intrigued. The eyes were sliced bananas, the mouth was a long, string bean, and the ears were upside down strawberries.

Were the green stems actually her earrings? Wow— her necklace WAS a string of peas. That's kind of cool.

Taken with her doctor's choice of artwork, Cookie couldn't help herself—she started to chuckle. It was cleverer than she had thought. Totally lost in her own amusement, she nearly jumped out of her chair when she heard the door slam loudly as her father rushed into the waiting room.

"Good Morning, Mr. Lcmon. Why don't you bring Cookie right on back?"

Wiping his brow, Jim Lemon nodded and hastily signed Cookie's name on the sheet of paper with the fat, red pen attached to it. Still breathless from running, he helped his daughter out of the chair. Then they both slowly walked past Ms. Liz into the hallway with the scale.

Cookie never felt more tempted to give Ms. Liz one of her glaring looks than at that moment. If Ms. Liz even cracked a smile, the second would've been brighter. After all, there's nothing that she dreaded more than getting weighed at the Doctor's Office—other than being made to feel invisible by the *Scale Lady*.

Cookie still couldn't believe that Ms. Liz uttered her first word when her father walked in the room. Her friend Chrissie was right! Ms. Liz couldn't be more opposite than Dr. Max. He was always so kind and so friendly! And Ms. Liz rarely was—at least to the kids.

Ms. Liz paused in front of the scale. That was Cookie's cue to take off her shoes.

What a drag!

She had that nervous feeling in her stomach again. For sure, mean Ms. Liz would have a comment on her weight. After remembering how much she had eaten yesterday, there was no doubt in her mind that she was "up" a few pounds.

Here it goes...

As Cookie started to place her right foot onto the scale, Ms. Liz noticed that she was having a trying time balancing without the support of her father's arm. She looked down at Cookie over her glasses and in her heavy brogue said, "Dear, why don't you have your Dad help you into the first room on the left. I can see that you're having a hard time standing. We'll weigh you during your next visit."

Cookie couldn't believe what she was hearing. *Yes!* She got away with not having to get weighed! She couldn't have been more relieved. As Ms. Liz closed the door behind her, Cookie eagerly hopped right up onto the examining table to wait for Dr. Max.

Surprised by his daughter's burst of energy, Jim Lemon let out a huge laugh and looked at his daughter propped up on the table. "Geez, Louise! What happened to you all of a sudden?"

Cookie looked at her father and smiled. She hesitated for a brief moment and decided not to answer him. She was happy about Ms. Liz skipping the *weigh-in.* It was her little secret. No one needed to know. Not even her Dad.

A few seconds later, Cookie heard a knock at the door and a very pleasant voice entering the room. "How's my girl?"

Chapter Seven

The Magnificent Dr. Max

Cookie lifted her head and saw a man who was a mere shadow of her pediatrician walk in the room.

Could this be Dr. Max?

She couldn't believe her eyes! Her mouth dropped open as she gaped at the strong, leaner man. He looked so different.

He seemed taller than she remembered. He even appeared younger than he used to be. He had only one chin. When she last counted, he had three. He wasn't even wearing the tight white coat that popped at the buttons. Instead, he was wearing a regular shirt—one that seemed rather fitted, and a tie. He was so slim!

Maybe it's the coat. He looks thinner because he's not wearing his doctor's coat. No, that's not it. His belly is actually gone! He's so skinny! Maybe we shouldn't be calling him Dr. "MAX" anymore. Wait 'til Justin and Chrissie hear about this!

Jim Lemon was also impressed with the doctor's physical changes. He wondered whether he was ill. He certainly hoped not. He broke the awkward silence and greeted his daughter's doctor. "Hi there, Doc. You look like half of your old self. Everything okay?"

Dr. Max just laughed. Everyone thought he had been sick because he lost so much weight. However, the truth was, he had never felt so good.

"Thanks, Mr. Lemon. Good to see you. No, I'm perfectly healthy. I've never felt better."

"Well...you're sure doing something right! In all of the years that you have taken care of our Cookie here, I've never seen you look so fit. Look at this gut! You've got to tell me your secrets. I've got to make some changes myself."

The doctor understood how Cookie's Dad was feeling. Just a short time ago, he was almost in the same position. He was plump. In fact, he was probably bigger. But...believe it or not, he had always been strong despite his size. That's because Dr. Max kept himself busy and active. Like clockwork, he was found every morning swimming laps at the pool. It was not unusual to spot him taking his two huge black Labradors for a walk each night.

As he washed his hands and organized his papers and instruments, he willingly shared one of his big secrets. "One day, about this time last year, a light bulb went on in my head...I finally realized why I was gaining so much weight. I was eating tons and tons of French fries—even after my exercise sessions! Besides being so tasty, I decided I enjoy fries because they are crunchy and skinny. I love eating crunchy and skinny food. Don't you?"

Like puppets, the Lemons nodded their heads at the same time. They were stunned. Both of them could hardly believe that it was possible to look so thin and eat tons of French fries.

Dr. Max knew he'd get their attention with this story! With a smirk, he seated himself on his swivel stool and continued. "So...I went out and bought myself those little paper bags that fast food French fries come in and put green beans in the bags and munched on those. I still do. Think about it—they're the same shape and same crunch, just without all that oil. Sometimes I put carrots in those bags. When I got the hang of my new habit, I learned that any crunchy fruit or vegetable would do—even an apple."

Out of nowhere, like a flying paper airplane, a tongue depressor soared all the way over to the other side of the room and into the trashcan by the door. Cookie's eyes followed the object and directed them back to the man speaking. He had a twinkle of mischief in his eyes as he grinned.

Cookie laughed at her doctor's new, playful behavior and almost fell off the table. She got hold of herself, brushed her bangs away from her face, and gave her doctor all of her attention. She had better watch and listen carefully. Who knew what trick he was going to play next? He always had a surprise up his sleeve—especially when he was trying to teach his kids and their parents something important. That was what was so fun about going to see Dr. Max!

Satisfied with knowing that his shenanigans had worked once again, he looked them both in the eyes and ended his story by saying, "Now...would you believe that I hardly eat anything with oil and I'm rarely hungry anymore? The secret about food with a lot of oil is that you end up eating way more than you would because you don't feel full. Yeah, it's been about a year now."

Jim Lemon started thinking about his own visit with his doctor the night before. Certainly, it was not as entertaining. Last evening he actually caught himself yawning a few times—even though he became frightened when it finally clicked that he was in bad shape. Now that he really thought about it, he remembered Dr. Morgan drawing sketches of pyramids and saying something about loading up on fruit and vegetables too.

Yes, he could relate to what Dr. Max was saying. He should start eating healthier himself. *Green beans in fry bags?* Anything's possible after seeing what he just saw! He shook his head and laughed as he imagined the professional-looking man standing before him, the one who had just flipped a wooden stick over to the other side of the room, munch on green beans out of little paper bags. This time Jim Lemon got the message!

Dr. Max thrived on talking to his patients and their parents. He really loved to see them laugh. When he glanced at his watch, he saw that time was running away. There were so many other families waiting to see him that morning. He immediately turned all of his attention to the young girl propped up on the table. "So, Cookie, I hear that you're quite the star."

Cookie just stared at her Doctor. This man really amazed her. He actually knew about her role in the play. How cool was that?

What a morning! His silly games were as funny as ever. They made up for Nurse Liz's testy personality in a big way. She even had a different doctor. His office may not have changed since last year, but he sure had! Nothing Dr. Max did surprised her anymore. Absolutely nothing!

When he gave her his all-too-familiar, warm smile, she finally answered. "Dr. Max! How did you know about me being Annie?"

"I bumped into your English teacher in the vegetable aisle at the grocery store last night."

"Really?"

Cookie was so surprised to learn that *her* doctor actually had *talked* to *her* English teacher. "You know *Ms. Martiss?* She's like my favorite teacher!"

"Small town, isn't it? Connie's been a friend of mine for years."

"Is she your girlfriend?" asked Cookie.

Jim Lemon was embarrassed by his daughter's nosiness. She was becoming more and more like her mother every day. *"Cookie!* That is none of your business!"

The doctor pretended that he didn't hear his patient's question. He never talked much about himself. He could be the friendliest person in the world, but he definitely had a way of keeping his personal life...well, personal!

He smoothly shifted the topic of conversation back to Cookie as he guided her legs up onto the examining table. "Ms. Martiss is quite proud of you. You know that, don't you? I'm just sorry to see you in so much discomfort. She'll also be sorry when she finds out that you had an accident. Your mother called me and told me all about it earlier this morning. Now...let me see that ankle."

The sound of the heater in the office seemed so loud compared to the silence that overtook the room as Dr. Max carefully examined Cookie's ankle. He looked at her foot and poked at it in all places. The doctor lifted her foot with his hand and bent it towards her chest.

"Ow! That hurts!"

Then he moved it in other directions—to the beat of a familiar song.

Is Dr. Max actually humming an 'Annie' tune?

Other than giggling at her doctor, Cookie hardly flinched at all. Realizing this, he helped his patient sit back up and said, "Well, young lady. I think we have good news. You may only have a very badly bruised ankle. Just to be sure, I think you should go and have an x-ray taken. There could be a slight hairline fracture. I don't think it's broken. It seems that you can put some weight on it. However, whether it's fractured or not, I want you to stay off it for a few weeks–*and* at the end of each day, it wouldn't hurt if you propped it up on a pillow and iced it for 20 minutes or so. If you have any discomfort—the kind that keeps you from a good night sleep, I want your parents to give me a call. In the meantime, I'll tell your Dad what he should give you to lessen the pain."

Jim Lemon was so glad to know that his daughter's foot wasn't severely fractured. However, he was still concerned about how she was to get around—especially if she wasn't supposed to walk on it. How was she going to make her way on the stage? "Hey doc. I'm glad to hear that Cookie's not as bad as we thought, but she still has trouble walking. We had a tough time walking from the car to your office this morning."

Cookie shook her head. "No Daddy. You just didn't want me to walk this morning. You were in too much of a hurry to get us here on time."

She turned to Dr. Max and said, "Yes, it hurts. But I think I can still walk on it. We're just reading parts from Annie for a month or so. I'll be okay to try out for cheerleading next week, right? Ms. Martiss said that I have to get a permission slip from you...if that's okay."

Dr. Max shook his head. "No, I don't think so. Even if it's a sprain, I don't think you'll be able to jump with your foot the way it is for another two-three weeks. Are you still on the swim team?"

With her fingers crossed behind her back, and her eyes to the floor, Cookie nodded her head. She knew she wasn't telling Dr. Max the whole truth, and she wasn't feeling proud about it. Ever since she made the play, she was counting the days until she could quit the swim team.

As if he had read her mind, the doctor said, "That's great. Never quit! I never did. If you're careful not to slip getting to and from the pool, you should be able to swim with your sore ankle. Swimming won't be hard on your bones and joints. It'll also help keep you fit."

The doctor stood up and walked over to the door. Before leaving the room, he felt he should share another one his secrets. "It's very important to keep *actively active*. That sounds funny doesn't it? Many kids don't get enough **active activity**. Do you know what I mean by that?"

Cookie shrugged her shoulders and said, "I guess so."

Dr. Max carefully looked at his patient and observed a bright-eyed, healthy looking young lady. He guessed that she might have gained at least 10 pounds since he had seen her last year. With great concern, he explained, "If you're sitting watching TV, emailing your friends or playing video games, you're not being 'actively active.' I know sports aren't for everybody. Believe it or not, they weren't for me until I discovered that I was a decent swimmer. It is so important that you keep active—every single day! For sure, your bones and muscles will become stronger. You may lose some weight. You'll even find yourself happier more often! And... you know what—when you feel a little better, if you don't want to swim, you can always walk or run. That's something everyone can do."

Dr. Max paused and wondered if Cookie grasped any of his suggestions.

He really felt for the family standing before him. They were two peas in a pod. If Cookie kept up her poor eating habits, she would end up looking like a miniature Jim Lemon in no time. He must also talk to her about healthy eating. He thought for another moment but decided to wait for the next visit. He cleared his throat and said, "First things first...let me get a set of crutches. Using the crutches will guarantee that you'll stay off your foot. If the x-ray shows that you have a fracture, the docs at the hospital will fit you with something like an air cast and I'll have to check up on you in a couple of days. If it's a simpler problem and I don't hear from you for any reason, I definitely want to see you in three weeks. Remember...no cheerleading."

Chapter Eight

The New Routine

Two weeks down and one more to go. When Dr. Max handed her the crutches, Cookie thought it would be a cool thing—kind of like being the first one to get braces or wear glasses in third grade—and for a day or two, it was—especially when she learned that she only had a sprained ankle. When she first returned to school, she adored the attention she was receiving from both her friends and her teachers. Now, giving up those crutches couldn't happen soon enough. Cookie had been counting every single minute of each day until she would be going back to the doctor's office. Besides getting rid of the crutches, she couldn't wait to see what silly game Dr. Max would play next.

Since her last visit, she had been hobbling on crutches through the halls of her school, through the rooms of her home and through the practice sessions of *Annie.* Her doctor was right! Cheerleading was definitely out of the question. If she could hardly walk, how was she ever possibly going to jump? Of course, Cookie didn't mind one bit. She got away with not having to wear those pesky, gym shorts that rode up no matter how she moved.

Still, life wasn't easy for her these days. Not fun at all! Getting around school was tougher than she ever imagined. Her locker seemed like it was tucked away and hidden miles and miles from most of her classes. The slippery, narrow, overly stuffy, and humid hallway leading to the girls' locker room had to be her worst trip of each day.

Knowing that a cool, refreshing pool was waiting for her on the other side was what kept her going every afternoon. She never dreamed that swimming laps would make her feel so good—even only after a week! Dr. Max told her she'd have more energy and feel better if she kept to her swimming. And she did! Again, he was right! He must really know his stuff!

Much to her dismay, rehearsals for *Annie* were scheduled at 4:30 on Monday through Thursday and Saturday afternoons. It took a bigger chunk out of her time than she thought. She was expected to keep up with her swimming, attend rehearsals, and finish her homework. Somehow, in between all of that, she had to get dressed and grab a bite to eat. Hopping around on crutches throughout the long day at school along with the extra exercise made her so hungry.

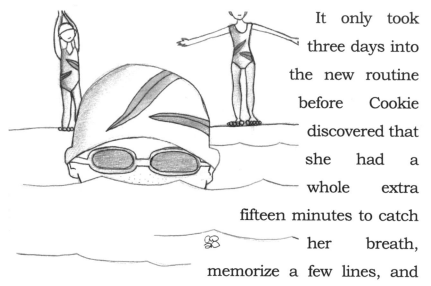

It only took three days into the new routine before Cookie discovered that she had a whole extra fifteen minutes to catch her breath, memorize a few lines, and munch on her homemade snack before having to shuffle over to the auditorium for practice. She was so relieved—for as long as she was allowed to be. It only took three more days before Cookie's friends discovered that she was hiding in the dining hall after swim practice.

So much for those precious fifteen minutes of silence!

"Hey there, K. Can I join you 'til Mom comes and gets me?"

Cookie certainly wasn't expecting to hear Justin's voice.

What is he doing here? He's supposed to be at Karate now!

"How'd you know that I'd be in here?" Cookie did her best not to show Justin how annoyed she was that he had spotted her. After all that he'd done to help her, Justin was the very last person that should make her angry.

"I bumped into Ms. Martiss as she was walking out of cheerleading practice with Chrissie and Sara. She told me I'd find you here."

Without waiting for an answer from Cookie, Justin took a seat directly across the table. He picked up the little brown paper bag filled to the brim with raw green beans. As if it were a bag of poison, he threw it right back down in front of his friend and acted as though she had just committed a major crime. It was so unlike Cookie to eat vegetables. They've never eaten vegetables in front of each other before. Never! "How can you eat that awful stuff? You're not eating *vegetables,* are you?"

Again, Justin didn't give Cookie a chance to speak. He shook his head and continued. "Raw green beans? *Yuck!!* What's up with you? Are you under Ms. Martiss' spell or something?"

Is he mad because I'm eating healthy food? He couldn't really be that bothered by this, could he?

Cookie didn't know what to say to her friend. She thought a minute and remembered once again how helpful Justin has been since she's taken her fall. She had to keep her cool.

For the last week, he had walked Cookie to her locker after lunch to help her trade her books from her morning classes with those that she needed in the afternoon. It was hard enough walking with crutches. Carrying a heavy backpack loaded with books was way too much to handle all day long.

Justin also had offered to help Cookie plan her day. That was because Justin's parents had really been pushing him to keep up with the demands of the swim team and to get involved with other activities. Oddly enough, this all seemed to have started two weeks ago, shortly after that phone call from Ms. Martiss.

So, together they decided that it was best for Cookie to squeeze in their mandatory swim team practice right after the last class bell from 3:00 to

4:00 and before play practice began at 4:30. This way she could have a break and Justin would be able to join her and help her—*if* she needed help.

Maybe he's upset because Ms. Martiss said something to his Mom. I wonder what it was. Something big is bugging him.

And Justin's latest attitude was really bugging Cookie. "I'm under *nobody's* spell. If you really want to know what's happening here, I'll tell you. This is all part of a game that my Dad and I are playing. Did you know that he picks me up every day after school now?"

She calmed herself down and started to tell Justin all about her latest activities with her father.

"It is so much fun meeting my Dad after school every day! On his way home from work, he picks me up after practice. That's the best! Now I don't have to be home alone—at least for three whole months!"

Cookie's father was on a major mission. Jim Lemon decided that the hour or so before his wife came home from work would be *his* time with his daughter. Noticing how hungry she had been especially after such long days and so much exercise, he thought it would be fun to take Cookie on mysterious *food adventures*. After his visits to both Dr. Morgan and Dr. Max, he was determined to use this special time with Cookie in a way to help them both get into better eating habits. He secretly wanted his wife to pick up on the new routine and healthy habits too. He'd never confess it but even though Carole Lemon was slender, she really needed to get into shape. She never exercised and always seemed tired well before he or Cookie did and frankly, it worried him more than he admitted.

Making this lifestyle change was going to take a lot of planning and extra work. Instead of making sundaes together like before, Jim Lemon thought they'd catch up on their day as they shared the chores in cooking a healthy evening meal. After shopping, Cookie was going to set the table and learn to clean the veggies as her father experimented. Never having cooked much in the past, he had no choice but to dust off a couple of old recipe books that his wife had buried in their kitchen and pick out menus that seemed healthy—anything broiled, without butter or sauces and all vegetables steamed. He wanted to take the bull by the horns and make the effort to eat better—more nutritiously! He figured if he did, then maybe his wife and daughter would too.

Justin never imagined Cookie just hanging out with her Dad. Whenever he was over at Cookie's house, it seemed that Mr. Lemon was either working or lost in a trance 'channel-surfing' the television. "How could it be so much fun meeting your Dad *every* day?"

"Because it is! Since I hurt my leg, each day's been a surprise. Daddy and I are actually on an adventure every single day!"

"C'mon, Cookie. Be real. What could possibly be so adventurous? Are you hunting for your dinner in the forest or the jungle every night?"

Cookie didn't think Justin was being cute at all. Totally frustrated with his teasing and disbelief, she pleaded, "Listen to what I'm trying to tell you... please? It may not sound like fun to you, but my Dad and I are learning something new together. So, it really *is* an adventure. And as you may have guessed, it has to do with food."

In Justin's mind, food was always a fun topic. He finally decided it wouldn't hurt to listen to what she had to say after all. "Food? Did you say food? OK...go for it. Tell me what you guys have been doing."

Cookie shared more of her adventures as she chomped on her veggies from the little brown paper bag. "It all started that night we visited Dr. Max. After we left his office, Dad treated me to a frozen yogurt—as long as it was 'low fat.' The next day, we drove to that wholesale club in Grovetown and bought these little brown paper bags that Dr. Max told us to buy. While we were there, Dad also wanted to pick up some celery, some bags of baby carrots and green beans, apples, and pears, low-fat microwave popcorn, graham crackers and peanut butter. In the car on the way home, we munched on the carrots and talked about what we were going to put in our snack packs for the few days. I couldn't wait to try out Dr. Max's favorite snack idea—green beans in bags!"

Justin let out a loud cough and interrupted Cookie. It all sounded way too boring for him. "How could *that* be fun? And what's it with all of the healthy food? If I was on some adventure, I'd be picking up chips or ice cream instead of yogurt or vegetables any day!"

At this point, Cookie had no choice. She had to let Justin know about her father. "Didn't I tell you? My Dad had a bad health report from Dr. Morgan. Now Daddy wants to give, as he says, the *'ole college try'* by doing his best to make the right food choices for each day. He thought it would be more fun if we helped each other and if we each prepared a special goodie bag of healthy foods to keep us from being so hungry in the late afternoon."

Justin squirmed a little in his seat. "Wow, I'm *always* hungry in the afternoon, especially right after I get home from school." Suddenly feeling guilty for giving Cookie such a hard time, he sheepishly let her continue her story.

"And for the last few days or so, we've been stopping by the grocery store to buy this special kind of yummy whole wheat bread, fresh vegetables and fish or chicken to bake or broil for dinner. It's been fun because each time I feel like I am on a scavenger hunt! Daddy sends me out on a mission to find a certain extra thing or two that we need to have for the house. Last night, I had to bring back two of my favorite cereals to compare the ingredients listed on the outside of the boxes. Dad then told me to choose between them. I returned the other one because the food label said that it had too much sugar. Speaking of food labels, did you know there was such a thing?"

Of course, Justin shook his head. He never had paid attention to anything like a food label before. Why would he? "So...is that your latest hobby? Reading food labels?"

Cookie answered, "*Now* it is, yeah! I had no idea! There is so much information on that label. It tells you everything about anything good or bad that's in one serving of food. Fake stuff like chemicals or the healthy stuff like vitamins. Name it...fiber, salt, sugar, and fats. It's all there!"

Justin listened as Cookie continued to tell him how she had even quickly discovered her own way around the store. He was actually picking up some good tips. Interestingly enough, after her second or third trip, other than picking up food for Mr. Cat, detergent, plastic wrap or cereal, she realized that she hardly ever journeyed into any of the aisles as she did with her Mother. All of the fresh food, meat, dairy products, fruit, and vegetables they bought lately seemed to be in a big rectangle surrounding the aisles of the store.

"I think I finally have this whole grocery thing down pretty well. Dad and I are learning a lot and we're having fun together. But it's not been easy at all! Do you know hard it is to pass up *free* cookie samples? I *love* cookies! And do you know what's hard? Leaving the store without the candy in the racks by the checkout lines talking to me. That candy is always talking to me! It really screamed at me after I bumped into Sara Webber last night. She offered to give me her extra bag of chocolate nuggets that she got from the 2 for 1 sale."

She paused for a moment, thinking, "You know, she would have gotten me if Chrissie hadn't been there. I started to take one of those candies and she put a hand out and pretty much grabbed it from me! She's really been looking out for me too!"

The longest minute passed as Justin simply sat and stared after his friend gave the run-down on her new routine with her father. He was ashamed for giving her such a hard time—especially after hearing how Sara Webber tormented Cookie too. Part of him was sad that Cookie wasn't around to hang out after school to do the kind of stuff that they normally did together. They had so much fun

eating fries at the mall, playing videos, and riding their bikes to get candy or pop at the corner store.

Yet another part of him was so happy for her. Justin would never admit it, but his mother was right. Finally, Cookie was able to spend more time with her father. Before, Mr. and Mrs. Lemon never seemed to be home with their daughter. This new routine was a good one for his friend.

"Earth calling Justin Gordon! Are you there?"

"Oh, sorry. Hey K, I'm really sorry about throwing that bag back 'atcha. I guess that really wasn't cool. Let me taste one of those things. My Mom eats these things raw just like this all the time."

Cookie wasn't one bit surprised when Justin told her that his mother ate vegetables. She thought Mrs. Gordon always looked so nice and so fit. Whenever she visited Justin at his house, Mrs. Gordon usually bragged about her tennis game or chattered about how much she enjoyed her long walks in the neighborhood.

Cookie picked up the bag filled with green beans and made a point to hand it politely hand back to Justin. He then examined the bag, singled out a small, skinny bean and decided to smell it before placing it in his mouth.

"Oh, Justin, it's no big deal! Of course, it doesn't smell like anything. Just eat it. Once you have a couple, you get used to the taste. Plus, they fill you up. Carrots, celery, apples, and pears are just as good. Actually, I think green beans are the best to snack on only because they won't get mushy. Better than anything else, I never seem to get tired anymore. For some reason, the candy bars and cookies always made me tired. Just remembering how tired I get is what helps me pass them up at the grocery store. Now that I've been drinking lots of water and eating so much extra fruit and vegetables, I feel really good...like I have more energy or something. It's okay! Try it!"

"You sound just like Miss Martiss."

"No I don't. I probably sound just like Dr. Max though! He taught my Dad and me all of this stuff when he checked out my foot a couple of weeks ago. We sort of stole some of his secrets."

Cookie then interrupted herself. How could she forget to share the latest scoop! *"Oh My Gosh!* Wait 'til you see how skinny he got! You'll never recognize him. He must've lost a ton! And his stomach's as flat as a board! *He's* the one who gave us the idea about the green beans 'n bags. Dr. Max told us that eating the beans in bags is what helped him lose his weight."

With a devilish grin, Justin said, "Hey, wait a minute! Maybe they *know* each other! Maybe we should be calling her *Ms. Mysterious."*

Cookie's jaw dropped. *Does he have ESP or what?*

"How in the world did you guess that one? Not only do they know each other, but also I think they're friends—if you know what I mean. He kind of told me they were."

Cookie's head was always in the clouds. Justin had known that ever since they were little. He just shook his head and laughed. "C'mon, K. I was kidding again and just putting two and two together. Whether they're friends or not, they're both skinny now. So, they exercise! So they both like to talk about how good vegetables are for you! Mom always does too.

But that doesn't count. Oh well, maybe I should cave in and try these things. Here goes nothing..."

Justin closed his eyes, placed the bean in his mouth, and started to chew. Cookie wanted so badly to laugh. But she kept it together after quickly reminding herself that she was just as "green" with the beans only two weeks earlier.

Cookie watched him carefully. "Well? What do you think?"

"Well...I like the crunch more than how it tastes. I don't know...it still tastes a lot like cotton to me. Let me try another."

Justin grabbed two more beans out of the bag and started chomping away. Then he grabbed the bag itself, held it in his lap, and began grumbling about

the massive amount of homework that was due in Science class the next day.

Cookie was flabbergasted. He stole her snack *and* it was disappearing right before her eyes! Justin, the one who hated vegetables, was mindlessly munching on green beans as if he ate them every day.

He likes them and doesn't even know it!

Cookie grabbed her crutches and quickly shuffled toward the cafeteria door. She was already a minute or two late for play practice. She turned around to face her friend, cleared her throat to get his attention, and said, "I'm off for the night. See ya' later, alligator."

Amazing! He was still chomping away. As she left the room, Cookie yelled behind her, "Hey Justin! *Now* look who's under the spell!"

Chapter Nine

The Baited Rehearsal

"Break time! Grab a snack, take a seat, and take a breath. In five minutes, we're going to do another read with the script. Believe me; you'll all be saying those lines in your sleep by the end of the term! Cookie Lemon...oh...Annie, hang on a second, I need to talk to you. Mikcy Downey, Daddy Warbucks don't go anywhere. I need to talk to you too!"

Relieved to know that she could escape for a few minutes from Mr. Roberts' nitpicking rehearsal notes, Sara Webber huffed with exasperation as she walked over to the snack table to pick up a can of pop and a bag of chips. Memorizing the lines and learning the songs were taking forever. To her, these weeks of play practice seemed more like boot camp. She wondered if she would have had more fun if she got to be Annie, the spunky and optimistic red-headed orphan. She also wondered why Mr. Roberts, the music teacher, casted her as the mean

Miss Hannigan. The idea of playing Grace Farrell, Daddy Warbucks' faithful, starry-eyed secretary, sat better with her than having to pretend to be the unpleasant orphanage matron who threatens and bullies children. Sara Webber was totally uncomfortable!

After a brief song rehearsal, Mr. Roberts sent Mikey Downey and Cookie Lemon off to have their break. Sara watched them make their way over to where she was standing by the snack table. They were joking and laughing about the song they had just practiced together. And, still pretending to be Daddy Warbucks and Annie, Mikey D. happened to have his arm around Cookie. Now Sara Webber was *more* than uncomfortable. She was seething! Not only did Cookie Lemon take her dream role, it appeared that Cookie Lemon was about to also take her very first crush away.

Sara Webber forced her fakest smile and said, "You guys sound really good."

Cookie grinned and suddenly realized Mikey still had his arm around her. She looked a little sheepish as she stepped towards Sara by the snack table. "Well, we still need a lot of practice but I guess so."

Cookie looked over the small assortment of bowls containing potato chips, cookies, and cupcakes. Without thinking, she reached out to get a potato chip, crunching happily. "I think you are doing pretty well also, Sara. It's hard to believe how well you're doing Miss Hannigan. She's *so* not like you."

Sara nodded, helping herself to one of the cupcakes. As an afterthought, she reached for another one and handed it to Cookie. "Want one? Mikey's mother made them at the bakery." She smiled as she noticed Mikey watching the girls. "I bet they're the best. She always makes the best things at the school bake sales." She leaned over to speak a bit more quietly to Cookie. "And I bet MIKEY would appreciate it."

Cookie giggled softly when Sara said that, and looked at the cupcake. It sure *did* look good. Chocolate cake, with a white butter-cream frosting and rainbow sprinkles for decoration. She was about to eat it when that little voice inside her head reminded her she was eating healthy now. As much as she wanted the cupcake, instead of seeing chocolate, frosting, and candy sprinkles, she imagined the cupcake was in a package, with a food label on it. She started to think of fats, carbohydrates, sugars and other empty calories that

might appear on that food label. Suddenly she didn't want the cupcake anymore.

Cookie sighed and looked over at Mikey. "I'm sorry. I just can't. I promised my Dad I'd really start making an effort to eat better. But it looks delicious!"

Mikey smiled, "That's okay. My mom will still like to hear that, especially coming from 'Annie.' Besides, it seems to be agreeing with you. You look good." He frowned as he suddenly thought about some of the things he had once said about Justin behind his back. *Now I know what Mom meant,* he thought. *About saying good things about people, and how it makes them feel better about themselves. Come to think of it, Justin's been telling us about eating healthy too.*

Sara watched Cookie put the cupcake back then sighed. "Well, I think they're the best, Mikey." She took a bite of hers, then turned to the table and grabbed a bowl of potato chips. "Well, maybe some chips instead then?" She held the bowl out to Cookie, who took a small handful and started eating.

Suddenly she stopped eating and looked at her hand. Her fingers didn't feel right and she noticed right away the oil that was collecting on them from the potato chips. Like a flash in her mind, she thought about what Dr. Max had told her, about how much he had loved French fries but realized how oily they were, and how the oils became fats in the body. She put the potato chips down on the table, then went over to her bag, pulled out her small bag of raw green beans and offered one to Sara. "These are pretty good too. A lot like fries, but no oil. Here, try one."

Sara looked uncertain but slowly took one of the beans from Cookie. Mikey shrugged and asked for one to try as well.

"Hey, these aren't too bad," Sara said through a mouthful. "Kind of sweet, really. And crunchy."

"They taste sweet to you? I think they're more like peanuts," Mikey replied and helped himself to another bean.

"Oh, you're right, yeah. I can taste that nuttiness." Sara took another bean as well.

Cookie's eyes widened. She couldn't believe what she was seeing. Sara and Mikey were happily talking together and munching raw beans! Dr. Max's eating habits were becoming an epidemic!

As the trio stood together, eating beans and discussing the play, Mr. Roberts called them back over to the others to begin rehearsals again. Sara took one last bean, hurried over next to Cookie, and smiled. It was sure a day for miracles—green beans being popular and Sara actually smiling!

Everything seemed all right again.

Chapter Ten

The Shadow

"Annie! Is that you? Hellooooo! Annie! Wait up! You're moving too fast!"

Cookie stopped in her tracks and turned around to follow the voice that was coming from down the dim hallway. She knew that the voice was looking for her. Who else could it be? Everyone and anyone seemed to be calling her *Annie* these days.

She wasn't used to being in school so early. It was very, very quiet in a creepy sort of way. Other than Mr. Eaton, the principle and Charlie, the custodian, hardly a single soul was ever around. Cookie was a little nervous to say the least.

For as long as Cookie was busy with the play and as long as he was in the building, Mr. Eaton gave Carole and Jim Lemon the okay to drop off their daughter an hour or so earlier than usual on certain days of the week. They needed the jumpstart to be caught up on whatever work they hadn't completed the night before. This way they would still have time to be together in the evening. That was more important than anything!

This morning was unusually dark.

It wasn't until the voice got closer that Cookie was finally able to make out the shadow who was calling her name. "Ms. Martiss! I didn't really recognize your voice!"

Breathless from rushing through the morning, Ms. Martiss dropped her heavy load of books onto the hall monitor's check-in table and took a sip of water from the very familiar plastic bottle she was holding—the one she kept with her all day long. She fanned herself with her free hand and apologized. "I'm *so* sorry! I didn't mean to startle you. Of course, you didn't recognize me. I must sound like a frog with this awful cold. *But...*I think we surprised each other."

She cleared her throat and began searching the walls for any kind of switch that could possibly give them a little more light. "Is it dark in here or what? Good 'ole Charlie must not have felt well enough to come to school this morning. This cold's been going around this place for weeks."

She gave the first switch she saw a try and light spilled into the office. Now that she was finally able to see things more clearly, she was also able to think faster on her feet. "So, what's up? Why are *you* here so early?"

Cookie didn't mean to stare at Ms. Martiss. However, the added light didn't do her teacher justice at all. She certainly wasn't her normal neat and perky self. She sounded horribly hoarse. Her hair was pulled back in a messy way, she couldn't look more exhausted, and she was wearing a torn purple coat.

Is this what Ms. Martiss always looks like in the morning? She never looks like this in class.

Cookie's eye also caught a button dangling from the ragged coat. She was too distracted by her teacher's unusual state to answer the question.

"Hellooooo? Cookie? I asked you a question. Aren't you going to answer me?"

Still Cookie didn't answer.

Connie Martiss followed her student's eyes down to her waist and noticed the button hanging from the worn out coat she was wearing. Embarrassed with appearing so disheveled, she quickly grabbed the button with one hand, pulled away the loose thread with the other, and placed the button in her pocket.

"Miss Lemon...now, I have to ask...do you have permission to be in school so early this morning?"

Cookie thought she had better explain why she'd been coming to school so early these past few weeks. "Ms. Martiss, my parents told me that Mr. Eaton said that it was okay to come early to school once in a while to hang out in my homeroom and catch up on my work. I think he's in his office right now. With the play and all...it's just been *really* busy."

"Of course! Where is my mind?"

Yes, Connie Martiss should have known. After all, she's the one who had been encouraging Cookie to keep up with all of her activities. How could she forget so quickly—especially if she could relate so well. She had been so very busy herself!

She shared with her student why she understood the need to have extra time at home and school to get things done. Lately, there didn't seem to be enough hours in the day. "It's no secret...I think you can see that I'm not quite together this morning. I stayed up half of the night to finish grading your *name* papers and, I confess, I slept right through my alarm. Of course, I wasn't about to give up my exercise—despite this nasty cold."

Ms. Martiss sighed as she took off her coat. "So...I am running later than usual. Hey, I'm lucky that I even remembered to take a coat. And thanks to you, I managed to save a precious button!"

Cookie smiled. She was impressed with how well her teacher read her mind earlier. Looking at the hallway clock, she was even more impressed that it was *only* half past seven. Then Cookie couldn't help herself. She did something she rarely ever did—she got up enough nerve and asked her teacher a personal question. "You exercise in the *morning?* What time do you get up? 5:00?"

"Yep. But today, judging how I feel, I should've given myself a break."

"Geez. That's way too early for me! That's way too early for any one!"

Connie Martiss gave a scratchy laugh. She loved this girl's spunkiness. For a split second, she actually thought she saw a bit of herself. *Oh no! Did I just say that to my teacher?*

"Cookie, I'm no different than you. When I have my mind made up, I usually get what I want. Isn't that how you are? You know...mind over matter! I learned a long time ago if I don't get my workout in first thing in the morning, then I don't do it at all. Even worse than that, I'd be miserable *all day long*. Trust me. You *don't* want a miserable Ms. Martiss! No...a miserable Ms. Martiss is not a good thing at all!"

Suddenly, Connie Martiss placed her hand over her stomach. The sound of her growling stomach echoed in the hallway. She was sooo hungry. There was no time to make oatmeal this morning. "I didn't have a chance to eat anything yet. Have you had your breakfast?"

"No...I'm not really a breakfast person. Neither is my dad. He says that it takes way too much time."

Connie Martiss was worried. Breakfast was a meal she never skipped! She was surprised that the family didn't have time for breakfast. It's not hard to grab a piece of fruit, a bagel, and a carton of milk as they walk out the door. Almost anything is better than nothing.

She looked at her star student and said, "No? You should *always* start the day with a healthy, nutritious breakfast. And I'm not talking about doughnuts and muffins either! Come and have a bowl of cereal with me. It'll definitely do you some good!"

Walking towards the cereal bar, Ms. Martiss threw her old, purple coat over the back of a chair at the nearest table. "You should never skip any meal. Lunch included! I saw you and your buddies *slip* by that lunch line several weeks ago."

Cookie was amazed by her teacher's sharp memory.

She probably even remembers what I wore that day!

Cookie dared not even try to stretch the truth. "We still had milk and rolls that one afternoon. That's something, isn't it?"

"I suppose...*but,* haven't you ever heard that breakfast is *The Magical Meal* of the day?"

Cookie just shook her head and continued to listen. This was news to her!

"C'mon. You can't tell me that you haven't heard that a good breakfast is fuel for learning. It's a great time for you to get all of the healthy foods you need like fruit, cereal, and protein to give you energy for the day. Plus, if most of your good calories are eaten early and if you have a good nutritious lunch, then you won't want to overeat when you get home from school in the evening."

Cookie thought back to the days before her new routine and to when her father started picking her up from school. She snacked on enough cookies, fries, and chips to feed the entire cast of *Annie*. Perhaps if she ate the eggs or cereal that her mother always wanted her to eat and then had lunch, she wouldn't have come home so hungry in the afternoon.

Now I've learned another new secret! If I eat breakfast and lunch, then I won't be so hungry. Or I'd still probably be eating that junk food!

Lost in her own raspy-sounding lecture, Connie Martiss motioned for Cookie to get her cereal and juice. Just as the girl stepped before her, she immediately stopped talking. Now it was her turn to stare. She couldn't quite place her finger on it. But something was *really* different. For the very first time, she noticed a change in Cookie.

Chapter Eleven

The Hand Trick

"Look at you!"

Cookie nearly jumped out of her shoes and dropped her utensils! She was flustered by another unexpected outburst. "Oh...Ms. Mysterious! No...I mean Ms. Martiss. You did it to me again."

Connie Martiss bent over and quickly picked up the spoons that tumbled out of Cookie's hands only to have them tumble out of hers. She was still hyper from the rush of the morning. And having a cold was bad enough. She knew that she had better slow down. Otherwise, before the end of the day, all of her students would be on pins and needles. "Ms. Mysterious? That's pretty funny. Actually, if I have to say so myself, Ms. Miserable is more like it— exercise or not!"

Cookie wanted to agree. Somehow, she had the feeling that she would be better off if she didn't. Instead, she gave herself a quick once over. For the life of her, she couldn't figure what Ms. Martiss was so excited about this time. "What's wrong? What did I do?"

"*Nothing's wrong.* I just wanted you to know that you look great! *Absolutely terrific!* You may not be eating breakfast. But everything else I see is VERY right! Your clothes are loose. And...no crutches! You were sprinting down that hall like there is no tomorrow. No wonder why I didn't recognize you before."

Now Cookie was stunned. Did she hear right? Her teacher just paid her a compliment. Hardly anyone ever told her that she looked good—only her Dad on special occasions and Mikey at play rehearsals.

At first, she didn't know what to say. But really, she didn't have to say anything at all. Her eyes did the talking for her. They were twinkling with pride.

Then she exploded. All at once, she spilled out every wonderful new change in her life. Her words couldn't come out fast enough. "My doctor said I'd be just fine if I stayed off my foot for a few weeks. And I did! Like you, he told me to keep swimming. And I am! I was supposed to see him last week. But

Ms. Liz told my Mom that he's been way too busy with those cheerleading physicals. She's taking me next week. I can't wait to tell him how much fun Dad and I are having these days with the beans 'n bags and how..."

Unexpectedly, Cookie stopped right in the middle of her sentence. "Hey! Wait a minute! You know each other! Did you see how skinny he got? And... aren't you two *really good* friends?"

Connie Martiss lightened up and chuckled. She was thrilled with Cookie's energy. But her nosiness amused her even more—to the point that she thought it would be fun to keep her in suspense as long as she could. "You aren't talking about **the one and only** Dr. Melvin Maximillion, are you?"

Burning with curiosity, Cookie swiftly nodded her head as she waited for Ms. Martiss to answer *her* question. But it didn't appear to be coming anytime soon. Miss Martiss only smiled and then went off to get her breakfast.

Ms. Martiss purposely took her time and s-l-o-w-l-y measured and poured *exactly* one half cup of fat-free milk onto the bran cereal. Then she wiped the entire counter free of extra spills and someone else's emptied packages of sugar. She even made sure that every tiny, single speckle of sugar was removed with great care.

It seemed like hours and hours before her teacher opened her mouth to speak again. "Yep! He and I are good friends! Actually, we're buddies just like you and Justin. We help each other out from time to time. Lately, we've been on this little health kick together. Good friends like to help each other. Right?"

Again, Cookie only nodded her head, hoping that Ms. Martiss would give her the real scoop.

Cookie then watched her teacher creep over to the other counter on the opposite side of the room to grab a tray, pour a glass of cranberry juice and stir her coffee. After she came back and *only after* she picked up an extra spoon and napkin, she finally said, "Nothing *more* than that, if *that's* what you want to know. Besides, not only does he have his children and their families to keep him busy and happy, he also has Maggie and Molly."

This time Cookie's eyes almost popped out of her head. Now curious more than ever she asked, "Who are Maggie and Molly?"

Connie Martiss burst out laughing. She got her! Knowing that she pulled the wool over her eyes, she had to confess. "Oh, Cookie! You are such a busybody! Molly and Maggie are his Labradors, silly! I'm sure you've seen him with them walking through town before."

"But...Molly and Maggie? What funny names for dogs!"

"They are, aren't they? I think I remember him telling me that he named them after his two aunts. Speaking of names, young lady, I really want to talk to you about your name paper. You wrote a great paper. However, I hate to see you so down on your name. C'mon. Grab your cereal and let's go talk. I have a really neat idea."

Ms. Martiss held her breath as she watched Cookie pour a mountain of cereal into her bowl and create a flood by topping the cereal with too much milk. It was only by sheer luck that the milk stayed within the rim of the bowl. Cookie had no clue when it came to knowing how much food was too much food.

Together, they carefully walked over to the table to eat. When they finally sat down, Connie Martiss decided that the name idea would have to wait. With Cookie looking so good, she really wanted to pass along more of her ideas about healthful eating. **But**...how was she going to help her? The last thing she wanted was to give her another lecture.

Then like a bolt from the blue, another brilliant idea came over her. She stopped Cookie just as she was biting a spoonful of bran flakes. "I've got it! Ms. Moderation to the rescue!"

"What?"

"Don't eat yet! You have got to see this neat trick. Lift your hand and take a good look at it."

Oh no! More Martiss madness.

Cookie rolled her eyes and reluctantly dropped her spoon to lift her right hand. Feeling foolish holding her hand up in the air, she said, "Okay... I'm looking. So...what am I supposed to see?"

"As I see it, it's a-okay to eat anything you want as long as you balance yourself. You know... **everything in moderation**. Load up on lots of fruit and vegetables, but keep breads, cereal, meat, and fatty foods to two servings a day. Have a little something sweet every day. But...that's only after you measure the right **portion** and after the healthy stuff is in you first."

Cookie nodded…"We're trying to do most of that now. My Dad packs me a snack bag of beans and crunchy fruit to eat every day before I go to play practice."

Cookie became more curious as her fingers started to tingle. Her hand was getting tired. Why in the world did Ms. Martiss ask her to lift her hand? None of this Martiss madness was making any sense! "Ms. Martiss…what does this have to do with my hand? *And*…what does my hand have to do with food?"

"Your hand will help you figure out if you are eating the right amount of food. Just humor me for a few seconds and you'll see. Tell me…how many fingers do you have on your hand?"

With that question, Cookie wanted to pack up and leave the cafeteria.

This is so silly. What is she talking about?

"Ms. Martiss, you know how many fingers I have on my hand!"

"Hold on. Hold on. It'll all make sense in a minute. Just answer my question. How many fingers do you have—including your thumb?"

With a smirk, she answered Ms. Martiss. "All right. If you really want to know...I have 5!"

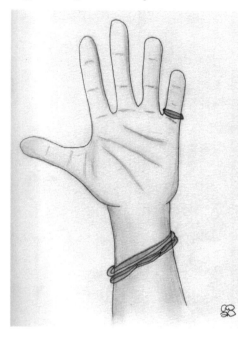

Pretending not to hear the sarcastic response, Connie Martiss just smiled. "*Very good!* That's the *smallest* amount of fruit and vegetables that you should have in a given day. **Five** servings. Now, do me a favor and make a fist."

Cookie clenched her fingers and made a fist with her hand.

"The fist is about the same size as a cup or one piece of fruit. Before you eat your favorite pasta or cereal, ask yourself, 'Is this helping bigger than my fist?' Okay, now pull out your thumb."

Again, Cookie did as she was told.

"The tip of the thumb is about the size of a tablespoon of peanut butter and the whole thumb itself is about the same size as an ounce of meat or cheese. Talk to yourself again and ask, 'Do I have more peanut butter than the size of my thumb smeared on my sandwich?' Better yet, open your hand, hold it up one more time for me, and look at your palm."

Go figure! This hand thing isn't as silly as I thought. I'd bet Dad doesn't know this trick.

Once more, she followed her teacher's request and stared at the palm of her hand.

"Your palm, minus the fingers, is about the same size as a three-ounce serving of cooked meat or fish. Ask yourself if you are eating a piece of chicken larger than the size of your palm. Any bigger than that, you're eating more than you need."

All of a sudden, Cookie didn't think Ms. Martiss was being ridiculous any longer. Her "hand trick" was actually pretty cool. What she was telling her really was beginning to make sense. "I guess if you're going to eat a lot of something it should be fruit or vegetables. Right?"

"That's right!"

"Hey, this reminds me of what Dr. Max said to my Dad and me about oily chips, sugary cookies, and French Fries. He said that they never filled him up.

But, the healthier, crunchier, and more colorful fruit and vegetables did!"

Connie Martiss was thrilled to see that Cookie wasn't bored after all. "Great point! The oily, sugary, or creamy things should be eaten in very, *small* amounts."

Cookie grinned as a thought occurred to her. *Oils! I noticed that when I started to eat potato chips during play practice! My fingers felt yucky because of all the oils on the chips. Kinda like the napkin test for the pizza we have at lunch sometimes!*

In her head, Cookie tied Ms. Martiss' hand trick and portion pointers to her doctor's 'not so secret everyday secrets.' She figured out that they were both telling her the same story—but in different words.

Yes! I can eat almost anything I want as long as it's in the right portions and I keep staying busy with active activities.

The sound of Connie Martiss' laughter woke Cookie out of her thoughts.

"What's so funny? What did I miss?"

"Oh honey. You didn't miss a thing! I think you got it all. But...you can put your hand down now."

Cookie's face flushed with embarrassment. She was caught daydreaming. This time...by her teacher! Bashfully, she brought her hand down and picked up her spoon to finish eating her cereal.

"Don't rush. It's time for me to run along. Somehow, the miserable Ms. Mysterious has to transform back into the marvelous Ms. Martiss before the bell rings. Want to meet for breakfast again tomorrow? I want to tell you about my big plan. No more morning lectures. I promise. It would be fun to talk to you outside of class, if you like." While she was speaking, Ms. Martiss pulled out a small notebook and began writing.

"I think I can! Mom and Dad have to go to work early again tomorrow. What's the plan? Can't you please tell me now?"

"Whoa...not so fast. No time for that now, however, I'll give you a clue...it has something to do with *your name.*" Cookie saw Ms. Martiss write down the date, the time of day and everything she had just eaten.

"Ms. Martiss—I have to ask—what *are* you doing now?

"Oh this? *"I Write What I Bite."* That way I know exactly how much food I am eating and more importantly what kinds. Sometimes, I even write how I feel. This past year I chose to change my lifestyle and decided that it could only be good if I *exercise* every day, take the time to *measure,* eat the correct portions of food, and *Write What I Bite.* Believe it or not, this little notebook keeps me honest with myself and in line with my new, healthy lifestyle. You can always write what you eat in your journal—you *do* keep a journal don't you?"

Having had enough of the guessing games and food lectures for one day, Cookie pretended that she didn't hear her teacher's question. She turned on her acting voice and jokingly begged her teacher to tell her. "C'mon, Ms. Mysterious. Tell me now! About the name thing, Please?"

Connie Martiss laughed. She loved the drama. But she still wasn't going to give in. She had to hurry back to her classroom. Besides, it was always so much fun keeping Cookie in suspense. As she walked towards the cafeteria door, she started to sing.

"No Annie, dear. Remember... *Tomorrow... Tomorrow...*"

Chapter Twelve

The Real Message

Carole Lemon felt like a schoolgirl playing hooky. She sat in her car and soaked in the autumn sunshine as she waited for her daughter to come out of the school building. She was thrilled to be caught up enough with her work. For once, she was able to slip out of the office and enjoy a perfectly delightful Indian summer afternoon. The trees were at their peak in color, the air was warm, and the skies were as blue as ever.

Carole Lemon was also happy to have a few quiet minutes alone before heading off to see Dr. Max with Cookie. The latest hustle and bustle of life was getting to her—to say the least. Her days were getting busier and busier, and keeping up with her family's new healthy routine took more energy than ever. With Halloween being only two days away, the opening night performance for Cookie's play was just around the corner. Time was flying by!

As she took her moment and sipped her water, she watched the other parents waiting for their children in the car pool line. Some were reading newspapers, a few were out of their cars visiting their neighbors in the caravan, and others were lost in deep conversations on their cell phones.

Like radar, Carole Lemon's eyes beamed in on the mothers that looked fit. Of course, she knew them all. Still, she gazed and wondered if at any time in their lives they didn't look like they had just come from the gym. She really wondered. How did they stay in such great shape and look so healthy? Did they exercise and eat the right foods e-v-e-r-y s-i-n-g-l-e day? She never gained weight, but she was always tired—way too tired to exercise. Did any of them feel like she did at that very moment? All of this healthy cooking and extra physical activity certainly took more discipline and will power than she ever expected.

That afternoon, Carole Lemon was hungry enough to eat a horse and she could hardly move. Her thigh muscles ached from that walk with her husband the other day and she hadn't felt this sluggish in many weeks. If she hadn't forgotten to pack that extra bag of carrots then she wouldn't have been dreaming of those chocolate-frosted donuts. She wouldn't have broken her new routine. It was hard for her to stay on track. It didn't make sense—she didn't need to lose weight! Why should she always feel deprived of the foods she loved? That nagging food diary!

Carole Lemon was just getting used to the idea of eating less of the sweet and fatty stuff and more of the healthful, natural foods like whole grains, beans, green vegetables, and fruit. Interestingly enough, she found them to be a lot more filling. Cookie told her that would happen. The secrets that her daughter and husband stole from Dr. Max were really working. Amazing!

Ever since Jim Lemon decided to take charge of the kitchen and change his routine, Carole Lemon discovered that he and Cookie had become closer as father and daughter. Both laughed all the time. They also looked really good—slimmer and healthier. Yes...she was relieved that her husband's red face and big belly were gone and more than tickled to see her daughter happily prancing around the house in her old gym shorts. She really wanted to feel as good as they did. She wanted to join in on the fun. The only way to do this was to jump on the bandwagon and be a part of the team. Little did Carole Lemon know that this was her husband's plan all along.

To feel part of the team, Carole Lemon made a plan of her own. Wanting some special time with her daughter too, she offered to drive Cookie to places that wouldn't interfere with the fun moments she suspected she shared with her father. Next, she joined her husband on his evening walks after dinner.

Then, the guilt took over. Feeling funny about not helping with the cooking, she insisted on getting up a few minutes earlier to make breakfast for her family. Her husband loved that offer as long as she prepared oatmeal or cereal with fruit. (And Carole Lemon secretly loved the fact that she managed to grab the easiest task of the day.) Other than that, she was sure to eat *only* what her husband, daughter ate, and only what was prepared for the day—including the green beans and other healthy goodies that were packed in the little brown bags. Easier said than done!

Nothing was going to stop her from keeping up with the new routine—not even her craving for

Downey's delicious chocolate-frosted doughnuts. No matter how challenging, she was going to do her best to prove that she could live a healthy lifestyle too. If it was good enough for her family and the English teacher, Ms. Martiss, then it was good enough for her!

Carole Lemon finally spotted her daughter and was proud to see her looking so fit. Cookie was skipping down the steps. Of all people, Ms. Martiss was right beside her. What a pair! Together, the two of them approached her car with enough energy to light up the town square. As she opened the door for Cookie, Ms. Martiss popped her head in the car. "Hi there, Mrs. Lemon! Great day, isn't it? See you, K. Oh...don't forget to say 'hi' to my buddy."

Connie Martiss shut the door and was gone in a flash. Before she had any chance to respond, Carole Lemon watched her hurry away to meet the group of cheerleaders practicing on the other side of the building.

Cookie fastened her seatbelt, gave her mother a big smile, and rambled away. "Hi! We went outside for gym class today. I can't believe Halloween is the day after tomorrow. It's too nice! Oh, Mom...we're starting to stage the second act today. I have to be back in one hour."

Between the two of them, Carole Lemon felt as though a twister had just passed by. She caught her breath and laughed, "Goodness gracious!

"Slow down! One thing at a time! Take a second and have a snack. I craved my favorite chocolate-frosted crème doughnuts and couldn't resist. So, I bought you a couple too—especially since you're looking so great lately. A little treat shouldn't hurt."

Cookie held the rumpled Downey Doughnut bag her mother handed her. The thought of eating one of those soft, creamy doughnuts made her mouth water.

Mmm, they smell so good...like they just came out of the oven!

She wanted to eat one so badly. On the other hand, the thought of how miserable she'd feel afterwards reminded her that no doughnut would ever taste as great as she had been feeling these days. That idea changed her mind in no time.

Because I'm feeling so good, I have to be strong. I can't give in! Cookie's conscience won. "No thanks, Mom. Really...I'm still full from the graham crackers, oranges and beans Dad packed for me in my snack bag today. I'll just drink my water until we get to Dr. Max's office."

Carole Lemon wasn't thinking. In her own, nurturing way, she was simply trying to please her daughter. *Only...*those doughnuts instead really played games with Cookie's mind and will power. After her own experience, she should have known better. If the doughnuts bothered her, then why wouldn't they have bothered Cookie too?

Despite the doughnut episode, Carole Lemon was still focused on Ms. Martiss' whirlwind, energetic escape to cheerleading practice. "You have tons of energy today! So does that English teacher of yours. Is she *always* that happy? And what's with 'K?' That's not your name!"

Oops! I forgot about that. Ms. Martiss almost spilled the beans! Good thing she didn't slip and blow the surprise. How am I going to get myself out of this one?

After scrambling awhile for a solution, Cookie thought the best way to keep her little secret a secret was to stretch the truth—just a bit. As if there was nothing to hide, she said, "It's really no big deal. I think she overheard Justin calling me 'K' one day and it stuck."

Carole Lemon wasn't sold. She pulled the car out of the school parking lot and prodded on a little more. "Hmm. I'm not too sure about this...she seems to know you pretty well for a teacher."

"We have breakfast together on those early days when Mr. Eaton lets you and Daddy drop me off. She's so much fun! I really like her. And she teaches me a lot—more than you'll ever know!"

As she took a sip from the water bottle she had tucked into the pocket of her car door, Carole Lemon realized that Cookie was right. Her own bottle reminded her of the one that the English teacher held as she was skipping down the steps. No doubt, Connie Martiss was behind her daughter's latest phase.

A few weeks ago, out of the clear blue sky, Cookie came home from school and lectured her parents on why drinking water was so good and how important it was to go easy on sports drinks, soda pop, and juice. Cookie claimed that Ms. Martiss said that the sugary drinks were full of empty calories. On the other hand, water was pure, a great thirst quencher and had no calories. The Lemon family had been hooked on tons of drinking water ever since.

*However...*if Carole Lemon heard one more 'Ms. Martiss said...' she was going to scream.

"That was fast. We're here already."

Within ten short minutes, Carole Lemon was parked in the lot directly across the street from the doctor's office. As they got out of the car, Cookie started to giggle. "You wouldn't believe what Daddy did to me the last time we were here. I was *so* embarrassed!"

Carole Lemon didn't even want to know. Her husband was such an actor. Anything was possible.

Together, they waited for the green light, crossed the street, and walked over to the building where Dr. Max had his medical practice. Much to Carole Lemon's surprise, Cookie politely held open the office door. After taking a quick glance around, she joked, "Wait! That's not Dr. Max's office. Maybe he moved."

Then she stepped back and carefully checked the outside of the door and spotted the familiar, hanging shingle. On it read the name,

Melvin Maximillion, M.D.

"I guess this really *is* Dr. Max's office."

"C'mon, Cookie, stop being so silly. Get inside. We have such a short time before I have to get you back to school."

They both walked into the waiting area. Cookie took a deep breath and recognized the smell of fresh paint. She looked around the room. Everything was *so* different. The overgrown plants in the corner were gone and the table with the fat, red pen attached to it was nowhere in sight.

Ah! Look! Dr. Max has all of his old Halloween decorations hanging! I love that witch. He's had that forever! Oh...yeah! I see Ms. Liz. We're in the right place.

As usual, Ms. Liz was sitting behind her little glass window. Underneath it hung a new sign with the words:

Please knock to let us know that you are here.

Cookie scanned the room one more time. Even with the Halloween decorations, the walls seemed so empty. Something was missing and she couldn't quite place her finger on it. As her mother knocked on the glass door to let Ms. Liz know that they were there to see Dr. Max, she took a moment to think.

Ms. Liz peeked out the window and smiled. "Hi, Cookie! Mrs. Lemon. Dr. Max and I will be with you in just one minute."

That was a first! She said 'hi' to me!

When her mother walked over to sit next to her, Cookie blurted out, "I've got it! I figured out what's different. The pictures! They're gone! The funny pictures with the fruit and vegetable people are missing. Where did they go?"

Carole Lemon shook her head and chuckled. Her daughter was just as dramatic as her husband. "It's okay, sweetie pie. Don't get so carried away. What pictures are you talking about?"

"You know...the ones that..."

Before Cookie had a chance to finish her sentence, Ms. Liz came from behind the window, opened the door to the hallway with the scale, and said,

"Cookie, Dr. Max is ready to see you now. Mrs. Lemon, you can come back with your daughter too."

Cookie skipped ahead of her mother and followed Ms. Liz into the hallway with the scale. Distracted over those pictures and feeling nervous about being weighed, she stared down at her feet knowing the cue to take off her shoes was to come in any second.

There it was. Like always, Ms. Liz paused in front of the scale and gave her that look.

Here it goes again...

Cookie took off her shoes and she stepped onto the scale. She squeezed her eyes shut and waited for the bad news. Somehow, it all seemed less painful if she couldn't see.

When Ms. Liz started to speak, Cookie thought she was hearing things. For the first time in years, 'the scale lady' was actually saying something that sounded good about her. "My, my, my young lady! Great job! There's only a two-pound difference from last year. Yes, ma'am! Two pounds less and almost two inches taller! Since you are taller that means you haven't gained any extra fat all. From what Dr. Max says, that's just about right for a girl your age."

She said great job! I can't believe it! Oh,...I have wanted this for so long!!

Ms. Liz was also full of surprises lately. During her last visit, Cookie didn't even have to get weighed and today...well, that was a story in itself.

Cookie opened her eyes and flashed Ms. Liz a great big smile. It felt so good to hear such good news. It felt so good to feel healthy and strong. She got what she wanted.

Yes! It was so worth saying 'no' to those doughnuts!

Her hard work was really paying off. And thanks to the special people in her life, eating right and keeping actively active ended up being more fun than she ever dreamed it would be.

And...when Cookie opened her eyes, she also found *the* pictures. How did she ever miss them? They were right in front of her! All of the peculiar pictures with the fruit and vegetable people were hanging along the hallway behind the scale.

Cookie jumped off the scale, grabbed her shoes, and asked, "So...why did Dr. Max move the fruit and vegetable people in here? They were much more fun to look at in the waiting room."

Ms. Liz smiled and directed Cookie and her mother down the hall. "So...you like the changes in here, eh? We're all changing these days. Especially the doctor! Feeling like a new person, he figured it was time to spruce up the office too. Okay Lemon Ladies...into the room on the right."

Cookie followed the older woman and watched her

swiftly straighten up the room. Just as she placed a fresh sheet of paper onto the examining table, Ms. Liz added, "Plus...Dr. Max needed the extra space to hang a few pictures of his own. Earlier in the summer, he was fiddling with his hobby. He ended up taking some great shots of his young athletic friends involved in *active activities*. He wants to show them off—once Halloween is over and our newly painted walls are cleared of pumpkins, witches, and goblins."

Cookie hopped up onto the examining table. "That's cool. But, why did he move them behind the scale? We're only in that hallway for a second or two. It doesn't take that long to get weighed."

As Ms. Liz was leaving the room, she glanced over her shoulder and said, "Good point, Cookie. However, Dr. Max placed them on the wall behind the scale for a very good reason. He wants us all to remember something *very* important...

...WE ARE WHAT WE EAT!"

Chapter Thirteen

The Treat

Perched up on the examining table, Cookie swung her dangling feet and played with the blood pressure cuff as she tried her best to wait patiently for Dr. Max to see her. He was taking longer than usual—and she was really getting bored.

After a few *more* minutes of waiting, Cookie's eye caught a flimsy, plastic examining glove hanging out of an opened box on the desk across the room. She jumped off the table, snatched the glove, and played with it after taking a seat on Dr. Max's stool. As she swiveled back and forth and back and forth and back and forth, Cookie blew air into the glove. She kept on blowing until the glove turned into a big fat turkey. Too bad she didn't stop, *because*...a second later, it popped!

"Cookie! Stop touching everything!"

Cookie didn't hear a word her mother was saying. She was too busy fussing with the fun stuff in the little room and she was way too pre-occupied. What

Ms. Liz said earlier really struck her. For some reason, she couldn't get *those words* of out of her head...

We are what we eat. We are what we eat. We are what we eat.

Cookie crumbled up the used glove and threw it in the trash. When she jumped back up onto the table, Cookie looked at her mother and asked, "What did she mean by that?"

Not having any idea what Cookie was talking about, Carole Lemon said, "What did *who* mean by *what?*"

Carole Lemon was completely distracted after watching her daughter fool around with every little piece of equipment in the examining room. She was also becoming frustrated with the time running away. There wasn't much time left before she had to get Cookie back to school for play practice. Dr. Max never kept his patients waiting. Something important had to have delayed him.

"Mom...didn't you listen? Were you out in the ozone or something? Remember? She said...'we are what we eat.'"

"Cookie, watch that attitude. I have other things on my mind like getting you back to school in time.

But to answer your question, Miss Smarty Pants, I believe she's trying to tell us that Dr. Max thinks if we eat mostly fruit, vegetables and other healthy food that you, Daddy and I have been eating lately, then we'll weigh what we're supposed to weigh—for our size and age. I don't know. That's just a guess. Ssh! I hear him coming our way. Finally!"

Just at that moment, the Lemon ladies heard a knock at the door and a very familiar, friendly voice. Dr. Max poked his head inside and said, "Knock. Knock. Knock. Trick or treat!"

"Dr. Max!"

What is he wearing? Is that a baseball cap on his head? Sometimes he is so strange. Oh yeah...it's Halloween!

Was Dr. Max at it again? Did he have another surprise up his sleeve? Hearing that Halloween was his favorite time of year, she should have known something fun was going to pop up today.

Cookie's eyes didn't leave her doctor as he settled himself in the room. He looked as tall and lean as he did five weeks ago. He still had only one chin. But, he was dressed so silly—for a doctor. Under his over-sized old white lab coat, he was wearing a

faded and worn baseball uniform. Dr. Max gave his all-too-familiar, warm smile and said, "Hi, Cookie. Mrs. Lemon. Happy Halloween!"

Cookie quickly forgot about those pictures. She was way too amused with her Doctor's wacky behavior and strange costume to think about anything else—even the fact that he kept her waiting so long.

My doctor! In a baseball uniform! While he's working! How fun!

Eventually she had to ask, "Who are you pretending to be?"

"Can't you tell? I'm a baseball player. I dug out my old college baseball uniform the other day. I'm getting a kick out of wearing it after all of these years."

Carole Lemon was really impressed. As ridiculous as he looked, Dr. Max's accomplishment amazed her to no end. She could never imagine such a thing for herself. In her mind, she never expected Jim to wear the size he wore in his younger days. "Are you telling me that you are able to fit into something that you wore over twenty-five years ago?"

Bingo! His shenanigans worked again. He had his patients in the palm of his hand. In his crazy way, Dr. Max wanted all of his friends to see what could happen when they ate right and kept actively active.

With Halloween on Sunday, two days away, it was the perfect time to sport that old uniform. No one knowing him just a year ago would ever have believed that he could fit into anything like that. It was a lesson to learn. For him, it was a great treat to share.

Smiling, he sat down on the swivel stool, glided toward Cookie, patted his stomach, and said, "See? I stopped eating those fries and wishful things came true. I'm in my old uniform! For me, those green beans and bags really did the trick! Yeah...that was it! Speaking of tricks, what tricks are you playing, young lady? You're looking very well. Just like the star that you are! And I hear that you skipped in here with no problem whatsoever."

Cookie didn't know where to begin, there was so much she wanted to say. Just like that one morning with Ms. Martiss, she spilled out every wonderful new change in her life. As usual, her words couldn't come out fast enough. "I'm still swimming—just like you wanted me to. I am keeping a food journal where I write what I bite. Daddy packs a little brown paper snack bag of beans and crunchy fruit for me to eat after swimming before I go to the auditorium for play practice. We stole that secret from you. What's best of all...he picks me up almost every day. We have so much fun cooking and shopping together. We hardly watch any TV anymore. There's no time for that. Oh, I almost forgot, my foot started feeling better almost three weeks ago. I hated those crutches!"

Dr. Max couldn't be any more pleased. Just as he planned, Cookie's father stepped in to help his family keep in line with healthier habits. He glanced down at the chart in front of him and said, "Well...it seems like it's been about five or so weeks since I last saw you. You are obviously exercising, eating the right food and definitely on the right track. Without even knowing, you could have easily lost a few of the extra pounds you might have gained since your last visit here. A healthy lifestyle is fun! Isn't it? I'm not saying it's easy—it's not! Good for you! Good for your Dad! Now let me take a quick look at that ankle."

As Dr. Max examined Cookie's ankle, Mrs. Lemon felt the need to add her two cents on how involved she had become in trying to help her family stay on a healthy track. Her husband seemed to be getting all the credit for her daughter's success. So, she rattled on and on about how they rarely stopped at fast food places and how they did their best to properly measure what they ate. Then she said, "Your little secrets have really helped us. We hardly use oil any more, we use those non-stick pans for all of our cooking, and we *never* eat fried foods. Oh, those snack bags! I love them! The beans and bags are the best! Amazingly, they fill me up. And thanks to Ms. Martiss, Cookie's English teacher, as long as we keep up with our swimming and walking, we realized that we could eat whatever we want to, even a little something sweet. You know...everything in moderation! Oh...aren't you two really good friends? I heard you were. She said to say "hi" for her. Didn't she, Cookie?"

In disbelief and as embarrassed as ever, Cookie placed her hands on her head and groaned, "*Mom!*"

Dr. Max laughed. "She *did?*"

Obviously, these Lemon ladies really liked to talk. Carole Lemon rambled on just like her daughter.

Dr. Max smoothly shifted the conversation back onto the family's success. "Keep up the good work!

You seem to all be working hard together. That's what it takes. Now...are you young ladies drinking enough milk...fat free milk, that is?"

Both Lemon ladies shook their heads at the same time. Cookie then made a face and spoke her mind. "No! I can't stand milk. It's so yucky. I only have it with my cereal in the morning. But I drink lots of water and lots of sugar-free pop."

Dr. Max was truly concerned for his patient's health. Putting all games and tricks aside, in a serious tone, he cautioned her. "Cookie, you just had an ankle injury. You are very lucky that you didn't break anything. However, if you continue to keep milk and other things like yogurt and cheese out of your daily food plan, then your bones will become weak. And, for sure, one day, you will end up with a fracture!"

Carole Lemon confessed too. "Doctor, I'll drink milk but I can't stomach the fat-free kind. Neither can Cookie. So...what are we supposed to do?"

He offered one solution. "If you can't stand the taste of skim milk, try 1%. I think you'll both notice the difference. You have to watch those sugar-free drinks though!"

Cookie was confused. "What do you mean? There are no calories in sugar-free drinks. I thought it was okay to drink that stuff."

The doctor shook his head and agreed. "You are right. They don't have very many calories. I've learned through my own experience that most types of sugar-free soft drinks fool our brains into thinking we need to find some extra calories to go along with their sweet taste. Believe it or not, they make us want to eat more. Not many people, including doctors, know this secret."

Dr. Max looked at his watch and didn't realize how late it was. That Halloween costume of his took up more time than he ever imagined. His patients' laughs and comments had him running late all day long. As he stood up to leave the room he said, "I've got to run off to surprise another young friend. Cookie, keep up the good work! You are doing great. Before I go, is there anything else you'd like to ask me?"

Cookie thought for a second and said, "Yep. As a matter of fact, there is."

Carole Lemon was really getting antsy. They were already more than five minutes late for practice. She nudged her daughter's arm and said, "C'mon, Cookie. Let's go. We've taken enough of the doctor's time. He's way too busy to answer any more questions."

Dr. Max was never too busy for *any* of his patients, especially the smart and curious young friends like Cookie. It was his job! He lingered by the doorway for a little longer and encouraged Cookie to ask her question. "What is it that you would like to know?"

"Would you like to come and see my play? Opening night is exactly three weeks away."

This time, Dr. Max was the one taken by surprise. He was caught off guard and truly touched. "Wow! Thanks for asking me. If I'm free, I would like very much to come. Let's just hope that I'm not *on call* that evening. If I'm not, I'll certainly be there!"

They all walked into the hallway with the scale. As he turned to enter another examining room, he tipped his baseball cap at Cookie and teasingly said, "Hey...watch those goblins this weekend! Go easy on that candy! And...if I don't see you before the play...break a leg!"

Chapter Fourteen

The Mindful Meal

It was 2:59, one minute before the 3:00 dismissal bell. The notorious "tap, tap, tap" sound was heard on the loudspeaker. Mr. Eaton was about to make his late-afternoon announcement.

May I have your attention please...

There will be no swim practice this afternoon. I repeat...

Swim practice is canceled today.

This time, Mr. Eaton's announcement was far from routine and totally unexpected. Justin Gordon couldn't believe it. The slamming sounds of the lockers along with the bantering and bustling activity of the main hallway caused Justin to doubt his ears. Did he hear right? Could it really be true? Coach Callahan never ever cancels swim practice. Something *really* must be wrong.

Justin scanned the hallway and managed to catch Chrissie Perkins as she was running off to cheerleading practice. "Hey, Chrissie! Did you hear

Mr. E's announcement? Did he say that the pool was closed today?"

Chrissie stopped to re-tie one of her tennis shoe laces. "Oh, Justin...that's old news. You really *are* out of the loop. The pool's been shut down all day. K told me that, three periods ago. See ya."

As Chrissie vanished around the corner, Justin lingered at his locker to decide how he was going to spend his newfound freedom. His Dad was out of town on business and his Mom was tied up with one of her tennis tournaments. He couldn't call his parents for a ride. So, how was he going to get home? The very last thing he wanted was to stay at school and wrap up his homework at study hall. It was *way too* nice outside to be held hostage for two hours at school.

Justin grabbed his gym bag, slung his weighted backpack over his shoulder, and hurriedly ran out of the building to beat the after-school activities bell. He made it to the car pool circle just in time! He was hoping to either hop on his neighborhood bus or ask a friend to take him home. But...he was out of luck. The line of cars thinned out and it appeared that all of the school buses had taken off.

Frustrated, Justin headed back towards the school building. He was hungry, tired, and doomed to sit in study hall until his Mom could pick him up. Thankfully, he remembered his emergency stash of last week's Halloween candy in the zip pocket of his backpack. He grabbed a couple of chocolate bars to hold him over until then. When he opened the door, K, of all people, flew out in front of him and nearly knocked him over. "Geez! Where are you going?!" Justin almost choked. "Don't you have play practice or something?"

"Oops. Sorry Justin. I didn't see you and that's funny, since I was looking for you. My Dad's out there waiting for me somewhere–and he called me to tell you that your Mom called him and asked if he could give you a ride home. We're really late. Oh... isn't it great that swim practice is off? Charlie, the custodian, told me that the pool's pump system was broken when I saw him early this morning. What a wild day! No play practice either. Mr. Roberts supposedly wants to work with Sara today. The rumor is that she is having a tough time with her Miss Hannigan lines."

Justin laughed at the thought of Sara Webber struggling with being mean Miss Hannigan and followed K to meet her father. How in the world did he miss seeing Mr. Lemon's car? Of course, he wouldn't have thought that Cookie would be leaving so early. "Hey there, Mr. Lemon."

"Justin, my boy! I haven't seen you in decades! You're looking mighty fine today." Justin ignored Mr. Lemon's quirky greeting. After being friends with K for so long, he was used to hearing his silly drama. "Thanks for taking me home. Mom's in one of her big tennis tournaments tonight."

Jim Lemon said, "I know. She called and asked if we could pick you up and I cleared it with her so you could have dinner with us." Jim Lemon was always amazed at the amount of time the boy's mother gave herself. From his point of view, it was certainly worth it. Wanting to help Cookie's friend, Jim Lemon said, "No problem. Get in!" As Cookie climbed in the back seat of the car, she said, "Hey...this is great that Justin's having dinner with us. It's been so long since he's been over. It will be much more fun having him help us make our homemade pizza, don't you think?"

Fun or not, Jim Lemon jumped at the chance to have Justin over to help chop the vegetables that will top the pizza. Although eating healthfully every night was great for his family, he learned that it has taken a great deal of time and much effort. Justin was simply thrilled to be invited. The last thing he wanted to do was sit alone at home.

"Sure! Thanks. What time should I text my Mom to pick me up?"

"Oh...tell her eight o'clock should be fine."

Jim Lemon still had to swing by the market to pick up the items to make the pizza. That along with preparing and cooking the dinner, the Lemons wouldn't be sitting down to eat for another two hours. Sometime during the visit, he figured that the kids should get their homework done too.

Before driving off, Mr. Lemon tossed two little brown snack bags of cut carrots and trail mix made with almonds, raisins, carob bits, and toasted oatmeal for crunch into the back for the kids. Justin grabbed his and dug in as if he hadn't seen the likes of food in weeks. He couldn't believe he was still so hungry even after eating those candy bars a few minutes ago.

"Next stop—the grocery store! We have to get the stuff for the pizza!"

Justin was also very curious to find that the Lemons were taking him to the grocery store with them. Cookie talked so much about her food adventures with her Dad, he couldn't wait to discover for himself why she was having so much fun. Until he learned about Cookie's new routine, he figured that like his house, food was just there. He never really gave it much thought as to where his Mom got the food or anything. Nor did he ever imagine that grocery shopping could be a family outing.

When they entered the market, Jim Lemon handed both Cookie and Justin a list and gave out his orders. "Cookie, sweetie pie...you get the lettuce—romaine and iceberg, tomatoes and other ingredients for the salad. And...Mr. Gordon, I need you to find a quart of fat-free milk, the smallest package of the two types of cheese on this list, whole garlic and a bag of baby spinach. I'll pick up a package of chicken and the special, fat-free tomato sauce to top the pizza. Let's synchronize our watches and I'll meet you at checkout aisle 7 in exactly ten minutes. Ready, Set...Go!"

All three ran off on their missions. Within thirty seconds, Justin found the milk and part-skim mozzarella cheese. Then he met up with Cookie by the lettuce section. Catching her off-guard, he threw a ball of iceberg lettuce right at her.

"Hey K. Think fast!"

Cookie laughed as she caught the round, ball of lettuce. With a gleam of mischief in her eyes, she looked around her to make sure nobody was watching them and threw the lettuce right back at Justin.

"This one's for you, Mr. J."

Justin was having a blast. He caught the green ball just in time and pretended to 'slam dunk' it into the grocery cart. He almost missed the top basket and they both would have been in deep trouble. The man in charge of the vegetable section was standing right behind him.

Cookie giggled and whispered, "Whew! That was a close shot. Let's get going and finish this list. Dad's waiting." Together they scurried around to get the rest of the ingredients for the pizza and salad, and were still back in front of the store in record time. Justin never thought food shopping could be so cool.

Jim Lemon unpacked the bags at home and saw his wife's note tagged to the pizza recipe. Mrs.

Lemon had thoughtfully let her husband and daughter know the pizza dough was ready ahead of time so that when they came home from their shopping excursions, the dough would be ready for them to create their dinner. Luckily, she had made enough for two medium pizzas so Justin coming for supper wasn't any problem. The other good news was now that there would be a few pieces left over to pack in tomorrow's lunch.

Within minutes, the Lemon's evening meal was under construction. As usual, Jim Lemon was the foreman in charge. He directed his crew as he walked outside the kitchen door to light up the barbeque. "Cookie, you and Justin wash your hands and get started with cutting up the vegetables for the salad and pizza. By the time you set the table, I should be back in with the grilled chicken and we can all roll out the dough and top the pizza together."

When Carole Lemon came home, she heard the sounds of laughter and the happy voices of her husband, Cookie and Justin coming from the kitchen. She could smell the pizza baking and was relieved that once again, she didn't have to come up with a nutritious time-consuming meal after a hard day of work. Having Jim and Cookie do the cooking was a great help and it cut down on the oily and fattening fast food that they were eating so often in the past.

After cheerfully greeting her family, he noticed that Carole Lemon went to the refrigerator to take out the angel food cake she had made the day before to get to room temperature. She also set out a bowl of fresh strawberries. After settling into this new routine, she couldn't wait to have a little dessert at the end of a day of healthy eating. That was her reward—and her family's if they saved enough room after filling up on their fruit and vegetables.

Jim Lemon pulled the pizzas out of the oven. "Mmmm...smells perfectly delicious! Okay guys... it looks like dinner is ready."

At that cue, Mrs. Lemon poured the water, Mr. Lemon sliced the pizza and Cookie tossed the salad while Justin stood by and watched the Lemon family in action. They were really a team. He thought it was so cool to see how they all worked together to make their dinner happen. When he joined them at the dinner table, he was really proud to see the pizzas that he and Cookie had topped looked like the real thing from the pizzeria.

Wow! No delivery here!

He could see the veggies and chicken toppings just steaming on the whole-wheat crust. It looked good.

This stuff tastes really good.

In fact, it tasted better than he expected too. Until that evening, he never ever would have thought to put chicken on his pizza. How would he have known unless he tried it? For sure, shopping was definitely an adventure. But, making and eating this dinner was even better.

The only thing missing in Justin's mind was a glass of milk. He was surprised that Cookie was drinking water. He always had milk with is dinner and thought every other kid did too. When he asked for a glass of milk, Mrs. Lemon poured him some—

and, remembering Dr. Max's advice about milk, she poured Cookie a glass as well—despite her squirmy reaction. Cookie knew that she was drinking fat-free milk and, she was secretly amazed that Justin was clueless when he took a sip.

How could he like this stuff? Knowing Mrs. Gordon, she's forcing him to drink it at his home. Yuck...

Justin never caught the difference. But, he did catch the odd and silly games Cookie and her parents played later on during the meal. Mrs. Lemon served her angel food cake and strawberry dessert—and everyone had a good time laughing and squirting on a little fat free whipped cream—the natural stuff, not the kind made with hydrogenated oil—as if anyone could even pronounce that.

Then strangely enough, Mr. Lemon pulled out a small notebook from his back pocket. Mrs. Lemon laughed and rolled her eyes as she pulled out one from her purse. Cookie ran to her book bag and got a bright pink one as well. While they were still chatting and describing their days to each other, each Lemon started writing.

"What are you all doing?" Justin asked in amazement.

"Oh, we are keeping our food diaries." Cookie answered. As if Justin was invisible, she turned to her father and asked, "Hey Dad, do think we had two fistfuls of veggies tonight? I know I had one today at lunch."

Mr. Lemon smiled. "As you know, we're trying to eat healthfully around here. So...every time we eat something we record what we ate, how much, what time and how we were feeling when we ate it."

Mrs. Lemon added, "Yep, it keeps us from eating junk or when we are bored or upset. Food is not a crutch, it's fuel."

While Mrs. Lemon and Cookie cleared the table, Justin quietly asked Mr. Lemon to explain more about the food diary idea. "Want to see what it looks like?" Justin peered over his shoulder to see what he was writing.

"It's not that hard and makes eating healthy easier," said Mr. Lemon. "Nothing like seeing what you put in your mouth to make you decide what is good and what isn't."

When Justin went home that night, he thought about the fun time he shared with the Lemon family. There was really something to their craziness. Taking

Time	Food & Amount	Feelings	Other Activities
6am	water		30 minutes on bicycle in front of news
7 am Breakfast	Oatmeal with low fat milk Raisins and a glass of grapefruit juice	Hungry and anxious about the meeting at work	
8 am	Coffee and fat free half and half		
9am	water		
10 am snack	one apple and an orange	Needed a pick me up	Delivered papers to Harrison's factory
11 am	water		
Noon			
1 pm lunch	2 pieces of whole wheat bread, lettuce, tuna fish with fat-free mayo, tomato, carrots, yogurt and orange		
2pm	water		
3pm	Celery and pea pods		
4pm snack	Brown bag snack of green beans and carrots with Cookie	Tired from the day	Carpool pick up and grocery shop for dinner
5pm	water		
6pm			
7pm dinner	Large fistful of Salad with romaine lettuce and iceberg, tomatoes, cukes and peppers, 2 slices of whole wheat pizza with tomato sauce small pieces of chicken and spinach 1 1inch slice of angel food cake, 1 thumb's worth of whipped cream and a small fistful strawberries and water to drink		Fun time with family and Justin
8 pm	water		30 minute walk with Carole
9 pm snack	1 glass of fat-free milk and 2 graham crackers		Reading

time to think about the food he was eating was totally new to him and the Lemons were proof that it works. He could see the difference in both how Mr. Lemon and Cookie looked and acted. For the first time he realized that K was way cute.

Mrs. Lemon was always sort of thin, he thought quickly, taking his mind away from some new and unusual thoughts about his friend. In his mind, he could see that she seemed to have more energy and just looked better—like his Mom.

There was something good about this eating right. He had already taken his first steps in improving his eating habits, now he was ready to take the next step of recording his habits in a food diary. Even those two bars of chocolate!

Chapter Fifteen

The Star

Cookie was standing in the wings of the stage peeking out from behind the curtain. The roar of the audience was too much of a thrill for her to miss. Amazing! The house was full. All of the people out in those seats were there to see

her perform. She was so excited. At any moment, Cookie Lemon was about to be *'Annie,'* the star of the show. And… she couldn't wait to shine.

Cookie wasn't nervous at all. She felt great and loved the feeling of being on stage. It was so much fun pretending to be someone other than herself. The only thing that made her a tiny bit edgy was the worry of wondering what her parents were going to say after hearing her real name in the role of *'Annie.'*

She was so afraid that her mother was going to have a bird! Maybe she should not have allowed Ms. Martiss to talk her into that crazy idea of hers after all.

But...I **am** *Kate Lemon. That* **is** *my real name!*

Cookie's eyes scanned the audience. Almost all of her favorite people were there. Well...almost all of them. She saw Chrissie and Sam Willis sitting in the row directly behind her parents. Cookie noticed that they seemed to be having a good time talking to each other. Her Grandma L. had made the trip for the play just fine. She was slowly walking down the aisle with Aunt Linda. It pleased her to see Grandma B. comfortably tucked in her wheelchair against the back wall of the auditorium. Too bad Grandpa Ed couldn't join her. Even though he was much too ill to make the trip into town, he promised Cookie that he would be with her in spirit.

Cookie looked around a little longer. Her parents were chatting away with Mr. Eaton. For a second, she hardly recognized them. They both were looking slimmer and spiffier than ever. Then she searched for Dr. Max who was nowhere to be found. So much for wishful thinking! When she noticed Ms. Liz in the back corner, she guessed that he probably had sent her in his place. Finally, when Charlie, the custodian, moved out from adjusting the spotlight, she came across Mr. and Mrs. Gordon. And...for some strange reason, the seat next to them was empty. Justin wasn't there. Where on earth was he?

He promised me that he would be here. The show is going to start in five minutes.

He would never miss this. I can't find him anywhere! And, where IS Dr. Max?

As Cookie turned away from the curtain to take her place on stage with Sara and Mikey, she sensed that someone was creeping up behind them. The lights were too dim to tell who it was.

It's probably one of the kids in charge of props.

But as the person came closer, it was Mikey who finally recognized who it was. "Justin! What are you doing here? You're not allowed to be back here!"

Afraid that he was going to get them all into trouble, he swatted at Mikey's shoulder and whispered, "Sshh! Don't talk so loud!"

"Geez, Justin," Sara recovered from the surprise, "You scared me so much that this wig almost came off."

"Well...I'm sorry about that." Justin shifted his feet a little. "I just wanted to talk to K before she went on stage."

Mikey grinned, tugging at Sara's hand and pulling her away. "Come on, Miss Hannigan. We still have a few minutes." He looked back at Justin and winked, walking Sara over to the other side of the stage.

Justin turned back to Cookie. "K. I never saw you this week. You were *way too* busy and always tied up with some dress rehearsal. This was my only chance to tell you to 'break a leg.' Oops! Sorry...I guess I shouldn't be saying that."

All Cookie could do was laugh. She was so happy that Justin came back stage to find her. She didn't realize how much she had missed him. As best friends, they shared everything—even the new habits that helped them change over to a healthier lifestyle. Coming out, as the lead role in her middle school play, was the most exciting thing Cookie had ever done in her life. It just felt so good and seemed so right to have Justin by her side.

"You are unbelievable! How in the world did you sneak back here anyway?"

Justin quickly explained. "Well, I figured that I had another ten minutes 'til show time. I ducked out of the auditorium just as Mr. Eaton turned his back to say 'hi' to your Mom and Dad. That was easy. The tricky part was trying to sneak past Ms. Martiss to get up those back steps. I swear she has eyes in the back of her head. She doesn't miss anything!"

Cookie giggled and couldn't have agreed more. "Then how *did* you get past her? What did you do?"

Justin snickered and said, "I didn't have to do anything. Dr. Max walked around the corner. When she saw him, you could probably say...hmm...well...she sort of got distracted."

"Dr. Max is here? That is so cool!" Cookie was thrilled to know that Dr. Max took the time to see her this evening. He didn't send Ms. Liz in his place after all. He really was her friend—and so was Ms. Liz!

Right at that moment, Cookie and Justin heard Mr. Robert's voice yell from out of the wings. *"Everyone...take your places. One minute 'til showtime!"*

Cookie became very flustered and pushed Justin off to the side of the stage. "Get out of here! Hurry!

Everybody's going to wonder what you're doing. Especially Ms. Martiss! She's coming up any second to introduce the play."

Justin ran off the stage and back down the hallway to the auditorium. The lights flickered for the last time. Out of breath, he returned to his seat with a few seconds to spare. Except for that 'you are in trouble' look his mother gave him, everything worked out as planned. He was as pleased as ever. He saw his friend and was able to wish her well. He turned in his seat to wave at Chrissie and Sam and they smiled and waved back.

"He looks so different now," Chrissie whispered to Sam. "Have you noticed how happy he is lately?"

Sam nodded, "I know. You should see him at the pool now. If you thought he was fast before, wow! We think he'll make the state tournament one year."

Within seconds, the auditorium darkened. Mr. Roberts took his position and the middle school orchestra was ready to play. Just as the spotlight shined upon the curtain, Ms. Martiss appeared on stage. As the director of the English program, Mr. Eaton had Ms. Martiss make the welcome speech for him. Of course, she didn't mind. She loved the glory of being on stage herself.

Connie Martiss leaned over the microphone and cleared her throat. With a smile, she welcomed the audience and thanked the people who helped with the fall play and made it all possible. Just as the drums were about to roll, she proudly introduced the show.

"Ladies and Gentlemen, it is my pleasure to present this year's middle school musical production introducing...

Miss Kate Lemon
As
'Annie'"

As the applause rippled through the audience, Connie Martiss took a deep breath and tried her best to walk off the stage as carefree as possible. She wasn't about to let on how emotional she was. She was so very proud of that young lady and for all of the positive changes she had made through the term.

Connie Martiss quietly took her seat in the audience—the one that happened to be right next to her friend, Dr. Max, and wondered if Mr. and Mrs. Lemon had noticed that, their daughter, Kate, was no longer 'Cookie.' She leaned over toward the doctor and joked, "Well? Do you think I'm going to get fired?"

Dr. Max laughed and whispered back. "Nope! Mr. and Mrs. Lemon will be thanking you in no time. Hey, what you did was the right thing to do."

Connie Martiss still wasn't comfortable. "Yeah, I suppose. But I should have given them some kind of warning."

"Remember, Connie, Kate wanted this change as badly as any of the other changes she's had in her life this year."

Connie Martiss was taken aback. "Did you just say Kate?"

Dr. Max leaned over and said, "Ssh! Of course! You just did too! That's her real name, isn't it? She's definitely a 'Kate' now, don't you think?"

Connie Martiss nodded. "Yes...you're right."

Dr. Max added, "Oh Connie...she's been dreaming about being Kate for so long. We all helped her to make it happen. And...just think...you also taught her and her parents another big lesson."

"And what is that?"

"Dreams can come true...IF you make them come true. Now...stop worrying. Relax and enjoy the show!"

Food for Thought—
Questions to Ponder

1. Do you like your name? Have you ever thought about what your name means to you and your friends?

2. Have you ever been teased? What does it feel like?

3. What did Ms. Martiss mean when she told Cookie that the busiest people get everything in?

4. Have you ever looked at your reflection in the mirror? If so, what did you think?

5. How do you feel after eating chips or cookies? Do you still feel hungry? Tired?

6. Do you eat as a family at mealtime? Does your family eat home cooked meals? Why would cooking at home be better for you than eating food prepared by a restaurant?

7. Why do you think Cookie didn't want to get weighed by Ms. Liz before her appointment with Dr. Max?

8. Dr. Max shared several "Not-so-Secret" secrets about eating healthy and feeling fit with Cookie Lemon and her father. Can you list them?

9. What is "Active Activity?" Why is it good for you?

10. How did keeping a routine help Cookie and her father keep a healthy lifestyle?

11. What kinds of snacks did Cookie and her family prepare during their new routine and food adventures? Why were the snack bags so helpful? Why is it good to eat fruit and vegetables that are crunchy and colorful?

12. Why is breakfast the most important meal of the day?

13. What does "everything in moderation" mean to you?

14. Do you keep a food diary? If not, why not start one and WRITE WHAT YOU BITE

15. Can you describe the trick Ms. Martiss used to help Cookie understand portion control?

16. Why it is so important to drink water and low-fat milk?

17. In your own words, explain what Ms. Liz meant when she said, "you are what you eat."

Afterword

Dr. Steven C. Shapiro threw the ball and I caught it! I never dreamed that I would run so far and learn so much. I will always be grateful to Steve for the inspiration, the encouragement and for giving me this opportunity. When he practiced Pediatrics in Northeast Ohio, he focused on empowering children and their families with practical advice that made sense and that they can use. Knowing that Dr. Shapiro has the same heartfelt concern with young persons struggling with obesity issues, I asked him to help me write this book and he willingly did so with great ingenuity and insight. To this day, I live by his 'words of wisdom.'

I was fortunate to receive additional professional support from Dr. Leona Cuttler, the Wm. T. Dahms Professor of Pediatrics and Chief of Pediatric Endocrinology, Diabetes and Metabolism at Rainbow Babies and Children's Hospital. I can't thank her enough for her kind and respectful endorsement of the book. A very special thank you also goes to, Sarah Lawhun, MEd, RD, LD, and the 'young volunteer readers' of the Healthy Kids Healthy Weight Program for their time and helpful feedback.

Many thanks go to a support team at Hawken School: Kimberly Brandt, the 7th grade math teacher and Kathy Fehrenbach, the Librarian for their objective comments and suggestions and Erin Thomas, the middle school art teacher for her creative input on the illustrations. I'd also like to thank Erin for recommending her student and my illustrator, Anna Lowenstein who graciously offered community service time with Hawken School to help me complete the book and bring Cookie to life.

I am grateful to my editors, Paula Kalamaras and Paul Kraly of Scribes Unlimited, LLC for adding the 'zest,' pulling the story together and keeping me on track.

A note of appreciation must also be given to my very first editors and dear friends, Karen Klockner, a professional in the book industry who held my hand at the beginning stages of the project and introduced the publishing world to me and Lisa Meek, MD whose advice encouraged me to empower *Kate.*

Thank you mother/daughter critique teams! These young friends and their mothers provided insightful comments and worthwhile recommendations: Alexis and Mona Anton, Christie and Cathy Beckman, Mary Kate and Joanne Feaster, Julia and Muffy Kaesburg, Sylvia and Irena Lasota, and Christina and Francine Vento.

My inspiring friends have 'walked the talk' with me throughout the streets of Shaker Heights: Diane Andrica and Jane Pinkas, my true and constant buddies of four miles a day, 5 days a week for almost 10 years; Lynn Shesser who took my first steps with me; Julie Raskind who 'opened the door' and, Sandi Brown who kept me fit and sane. Hugs to all and thanks for listening to my tale of Cookie Lemon!

A thousand thanks go to my other loyal friends and family members, especially my Dad, George Mandros, and my sisters: Annette, Pamela, and Joanne. These very special people know how they helped me along the path. I would not have come to this point without their motivation, support, and patient ears. And...from the bottom of my heart I want to thank my beautiful mother, Thalia for helping me brainstorm the book's title and for always being in my corner.

The greatest thank you of all goes to my devoted husband, Christopher, and to my fantastic sons, George and Greg for their love, and respect for my mission and me. I love you all! Because of you, my dream came true.

About the Author and Illustrator

Vanessa Pasiadis was involved in high school dramatics in Pittsburgh PA. She graduated from Chatham University with a degree in Biology and the University of Pittsburgh's Graduate School of Public Health with a Master's degree in Health Administration. She now lives in Shaker Heights, Ohio, with her family. A former teacher and health care consultant, Vanessa has turned her insights to helping young people lead a healthy lifestyle through good nutrition and fun.

Anna Lowenstein, a talented young artist, is a perfect example of Vanessa's vision of pursuing a healthy lifestyle through activity. With enthusiasm and skill, Anna illustrated this book while attending Hawken Middle School in Cleveland, Ohio.